PRAISE FOR *SILENT WORDS*
By Joan Drury
(Spinsters Ink, 1996)

"No mainstream genre author would write a mystery that is heavy on thought, light on action and wrapped up in events that happened 70 years in the past. But that's exactly what Joan Drury gets away with in *Silent Words*. . . . What this introspective novel lacks in urgency it makes up in character and atmosphere . . ."
—*New York Times Book Review*

". . . an upbeat, unusual mystery . . . a fine addition to the lesbian mystery category." —*Publishers Weekly*

"Drury . . . offers seductive prose, a caring protagonist, wonderful scenery, and small-town idiosyncrasies. A solid addition to most collections." —*Library Journal*

"Buffs of family tree research should enjoy." —*Booklist*

"This book has it all: a mature and engaging protagonist, local color and suspense, all woven together with a fascinating backstory that makes this one impossible to put down."
—*Alfred Hitchcock Mystery Magazine*

"Joan Drury's *Silent Words* has it all: determined protagonist, irascible cluster of villains, intriguing mystery, sound resolution and enough moxie to earn nominations for a Minnesota Book Award and an Edgar." —*St. Paul Pioneer Press*

"What moves *Silent Words* above the rank of one more feminist mystery is the care Drury affords her characters. In a genre that has no scarcity of streetwise private eyes who compete outside the law, Tyler Jones is a sleuth with substance." —*Duluth News-Tribune*

"Drury unravels this mystery in a deliciously tantalizing and completely believable way, and the denouement is quite satisfying. . . . In Tyler, Drury has created the sort of straightforward and strong, yet vulnerable heroine that one could envision Jodie Foster playing in a film . . ."

—*Independent Publisher*

"For anyone who enjoys the north shore of Lake Superior, and for all mystery fans, Drury's *Silent Words* is a must-read. This feminist telling of a family and a community and the secrets that are kept offers well-drawn characters in a style that's political without being preachy."

—*Minnesota Women's Press*

"*Silent Words* is a riveting read that draws you charmingly into its world. At the close, you'll feel you've had a delightfully satisfying meal . . . and you'll still want seconds."

—*Lambda Book Report*

"Not only does [Drury's] work provide suspense and suspense, it does so in a delightfully enjoyable way. Her style is polished and articulate, with a clear care for the language she uses so well. She conveys a concrete sense of physical landscapes . . . Yet it is Drury's internal landscapes that most impress me, that ability to put the reader into both the head and the heart of the main character."

—*Lesbian Review of Books*

"Ms. Drury turns her tale in so clever a way that you become hooked without even noticing. . . . The plot will thicken till you're caught fast by the hook Ms. Drury has been dangling. Then you'll have to postpone eating dinner or going to bed because you need to be sure Tyler comes out okay."

—*Feminist Voices* (Madison, WI)

". . . a compelling read that'll keep you engrossed right on through to the last page."

—*XS* (Ft. Lauderdale, FL)

"The sure descriptions of the Midwestern setting, as well as the many strong, interesting women characters who help Tyler with her investigation, make this book a pleasure."

—*Labyrinth* (Philadelphia)

"The mystery is complicated with an unpredictable storyline and Drury has a flair for narrative description. . . . an interesting and intriguing book." —*Outword* (Sacramento, CA)

"Strong on suspense and mystery, this modern-day tale flows from page to page. A must for lovers both of mysteries and feminists' work." —*Women in Libraries*

"Joan M. Drury brilliantly and colorfully explores family relationships, interactions between neighbors, and sexual phobias (especially homophobia) that makes readers want to relook their own personal beliefs and relationships. . . . Tyler Jones, in her second outing, is one of the better amateur female sleuths in '90s literature." —*Midwest Book Review*

". . . *Silent Words* is a mesmerizing, unforgettable novel." —*Reviewer's Bookwatch*

"Drury is an excellent writer, good with dialogue and with plot twists . . ." —*American Reporter Book Review*

". . . a thinking person's mystery . . . makes for provocative reading." —Amazon.com Books

"Recently nominated for an Edgar Award for Best Paperback Original, *Silent Words* successfully pulls together an incredible range of emotions about an incredible place in a very credible mystery." —AOL *Book Report*

"Throughout the novel Drury creates an evocative sense of place, with her well formed writing and attention to detail. . . . Drury carries us (and Tyler) along on the quality of her unfolding prose, to calmly and quietly allow events to take place." —*Crime Time* (England)

"*Silent Words* is a delight to read and a story that effortlessly weaves through the pages. It is also a refreshing change from the usual crime fiction in that this mystery is central to the main character, Tyler Jones', immediate family." —*Gay Scotland*

CLOSED
IN
SILENCE

Wherever you are, create community. Then you'll never be closed in silence.

Joan M. Drury

Joan M. Drury

Spinsters Ink
Duluth, MN

First edition published September 1998
10-9-8-7-6-5-4-3-2-1

Spinsters Ink
32 E. First St., #330
Duluth, MN 55802-2002

Cover art by Sue Pavlatos
Cover design by Tara Christopherson, Fruitful Results Design

Production: Liz Brissett   Ryan Petersen
               Charlene Brown   Kim Riordan
               Helen Dooley   Emily Soltis
               Tracy Gilsvik   Amy Strasheim
               Marian Hunstiger   Liz Tufte
               Kelly Kager   Nancy Walker
               Claire Kirch

Library of Congress Cataloging-in-Publication Data

Drury, Joan M., 1945–
    Closed in silence / Joan M. Drury – 1st ed.
       p.   cm.
    ISBN 1-883523-29-X (alk. paper)
    1. Title.
PS3554.R827C58   1998
813'.54—dc21   98–24115
                                                     CIP

Printed in the U.S.A. on recycled paper with soy-based inks.

Joan M. Drury is author of *The Other Side of Silence,* a Minnesota Book Award finalist, and *Silent Words,* winner of a 1997 Minnesota Book Award, a 1997 PMA Benjamin Franklin Award, the 1997 Northeastern Minnesota Book Award, and a 1997 MIPA Award of Merit. *Silent Words* was also shortlisted for a 1997 Edgar Allan Poe Award and a 1997 Small Press Book Award.

For Marilyn—
whose name is synonymous with
friendship and grace,
whose love and support have sustained me
(and continue to sustain me)
through everything.
May you receive from me
and the rest of the universe
double the blessings
I've received from you.

"Women's stories have not been told. And without stories there is no articulation of experience. Without stories a woman is lost when she comes to make the important decisions of her life. She does not learn to value her struggles, to celebrate her strengths, to comprehend her pain. Without stories she cannot understand herself. Without stories she is alienated from those deeper experiences of self and world that have been called spiritual or religious. She is closed in silence."

— Carol Christ, *Diving Deep and Surfacing*

ACKNOWLEDGEMENTS

Writers are often asked for whom they are writing. I have answered this question in a variety of ways: for anyone who likes a good story; for women who are looking for their stories to be told; for myself. But as I write more and more (and grow older at the same time), I realize that I am, actually, writing for the characters whose stories I'm telling. With that in mind, I feel—first and foremost—I need to thank my characters who "visit" me with such clarity, such vivid opinions, such certainty that I sometimes feel I have little to do with their "creation." They continue to demand honesty and precision about themselves and their stories, resulting in fine books, I believe.

Then, the usual suspects: the women at Spinsters Ink and Norcroft: A Writing Retreat for Women who not only make my demanding and complex life possible but also are crucial to my ever getting anything written. These women are: Zad Walker (the general slave driver and wide-shouldered support maven), Claire Kirch (the marketing goddess), Liz Tufte (in charge of production extraordinaire), Marian Hunstiger (fulfilling fulfillment amazon as well as detail queen), and Ryan Peterson and Tracy Gilsvik (also in charge of details, including research and keeping my life on track) at Spinsters, and from Norcroft—Jean Sramek and Kim Luedtke (the women who keep everything moving and, in Kim's case, keeps smiles on our faces) and Kelly Kager (the house "angel" to the residents and me, too).

I have to, further, acknowledge the actual work that the Spinsters women did to bring this book to fruition. Such a group of talented, bright, funny, fun women—everyone should get to work with people like them! Special thanks also goes to my editor who continues to love my work and insist it be as good as it can be,

Kelly Kager, and my copyeditor, Charlene Brown, who smooths all the edges and catches all the snags. And a fabulous group of volunteers and interns who do everything else!

Then my family—children and grandchildren—as well as extended family of friends and loved ones who bless me with so much love and encouragement, criticism and skepticism, informing every decision I make. Too numerous to name, I'll highlight a few: my parents—always, first, and most important, Barbara and Edward Drury; the "kids," of course—Allie, Mirranda, Kevin, Scooter, Karie, and Kelly; spectacular friends— Marilyn, Barb and Lynn, Pamela, Arlinda, the other Marilyn, Maureen, Zad, Nancy and Joe and Nia and Mavis, Ellen and Sue, Rita and Diane, "Uncle" Timmy, Roberta, Virginia, Nevada, Carole, Deb and Nan, Irving and crew, Deb and Ron, Geri, Libby, Deb and Tom, Paul-my-butler, and all the others I'm forgetting, including my first readers, stunning critics/encouragers (it's like having three extra editors and bosom buddies)—Pamela Mittlefehldt, Paula Barish, and Mimi Wheatwind.

Who else? All the feminists who've talked to me, taught me, inspired me, informed me, opened me, dreamed with me over the years. The University of Minnesota's Women's Studies Department for providing me with a fine feminist education (sometimes in spite of themselves) and also a good friend, Jacquelyn, plus lots of information for this book. The astounding women who shared Norcroft with me while I was writing this book: Carolyn, Nighat, Cressa, Joan, Hertha, Lela, Toby, Joslyn, and Audrey.

This could be endless, and isn't that terrific? I do nothing alone, nothing without the constant, continuous, sometimes unseen and unacknowledged aid of so many good people, so many good women. Oh, yes—and Linda, too. Absolutely, Linda. Who pushed me, lovingly, through the final touches.

Thank you to you all!

CLOSED
IN
SILENCE

Joan M. Drury

WOMENSWORDS
Tyler Jones

"Half of human history has been lived by women." These were the opening words of a lengthy proposal that a coalition of educators and students presented to the University of Minnesota's administration in 1972 in an attempt to convince it that we needed a Women's Studies program on campus. "Half of human history has been lived by women." It seems so obvious, doesn't it? Why did we have to state the obvious? Why, still, do we have to remind people of this unmistakable truth?

We got our Women's Studies program, opening on the U of M's campus in the fall of 1973. And for years, all of us involved had to repeat these words to those who continually asked—and still ask—"What about a Men's Studies' Department?" Again the obvious—the study of men has always existed in every department. Just look at the class offerings in many college catalogs: The History of Man, Man and Art, Philosophical Inquiry into Man's Nature—not to speak of the focus on male writers, male architects, male archaeologists, male "something" in every discipline. Men have always been the major subject of higher learning, of college discourse, because men, after all, are the "real" people. Even those colleges and universities that are enlightened enough to use nonsexist language in their course offerings still have classes like Major American Authors (all men) and American Women Writers (the "other" authors, I guess). American Men Writers is never listed because that is the "norm."

Even though women lived—and continue to live—half of human history.

Tillie Olsen gave a speech, in the early '70s, detailing the marginalization of women's writing. One in twelve, she informed us, only one in twelve writers included in anthologies, textbooks, "best" collections, or chosen to be criticized or reviewed or taught in college curricula, were women. That's 8 percent. As if only 8 percent of the writers in history (or currently) were women. Olsen expanded this speech to create her spellbinding and myth-breaking book, *Silences*.

Twelve years later, in the '80s, Joanna Russ checked our progress and discovered that nothing much

WOMENSWORDS

had changed. Her findings, published in *How to Suppress Women's Writing,* stated that between 5 and 8 percent of all writers included in anthologies, textbooks, "best" collections, or chosen to be criticized or reviewed or taught in college curricula, were women.

And now we're in a new decade. Have these numbers changed? Not appreciably. But, someone keeps whining, "Why a Women's Studies Department? What about the men? What do women want, anyway?" For starters, equitable representation.

The Women's Liberation Movement and Women's Studies, its academic arm, are a natural reaction to the fact that, even though half of human history has been lived by women, women—as a focus of study, as a serious academic subject, as individuals in the world and *history*—have been systematically erased, dismissed, diminished, ignored, scorned, forgotten. For those of us who "came of age" during the early years of this wave of feminism (only one of many throughout human history), this movement and philosophy not only provided a logical explanation for the vagaries of human activity but also became a way of life.

I entered the University of Minnesota in 1971 and was soon caught up, with my five closest friends, in this great movement of our time. Now, twenty-plus years later, I plan to attend a reunion of the six of us—women who lived together, demonstrated together, organized together, laughed and cried and fought together, stayed up entire nights planning the creation of a new, just society. We were the cutting edge, we were radical feminists: not interested in getting a *piece* of the pie, but demanding a whole *new* pie!

It's been twenty years since graduation, twenty years since some of us have even seen one another. It will be interesting to discover what impact, if any, the Women's Liberation Movement has had on our personal histories, how it is we've been living *our part* of human history.

In the meantime, I do the only thing I can: I keep putting one foot in front of the other. I keep moving forward—women's words propelling me on my way.

Tucked into Rachel's invitation was an obituary of Grace's father. *How odd,* I thought, stooping to pick it up off the floor where it had fluttered when I opened the envelope. The invitation interested me more, so I put the obit aside. Rachel wanted all of us—Teddie and Grace and Julie and Mary Sharon and me—to get together to celebrate the twenty years since we'd graduated from college.

Although Rachel and I kept in fairly regular contact, and Teddie and I exchanged the infrequent letter, I hadn't seen or talked to Grace for twenty years. Mary Sharon was my closest friend, the only one I talked to constantly. And Julie. Julie I hadn't seen since that day fifteen—no, seventeen—years ago when she "drove off into the sunset" with another woman. Julie. Did I really want to see her again? I guess the honest answer to that question would be—yes and no. *This is absurd!* I thought. *I can't possibly give a damn! After all, it's been almost twenty years!*

I gazed at the invitation. Rachel was proposing we all come to "the island" for a long weekend in early June. The island was in the San Juans above Puget Sound. Her family, established Minnesota lumber barons, had followed the railroad west in the last century and begun pillaging the virgin forests of the Northwest. Her great-grandfather had bought one of the smaller islands in the San Juans and had built a primitive getaway there. It remained in her family ever after—getting updated, modernized, and built-on, over the past hundred years. Back in college, we had always talked about going there but had never quite gotten around to it. Here was our opportunity, after all these years, to rectify that—and to reconnect with one another.

Mary Sharon. Teddie. Rachel. Grace. Julie. I leaned back in my desk chair, swiveling around to look at the photos covering one wall of my home office. There we all were, immortalized in color Kodachrome: Mary Sharon, in her "death" phase, dressed head-to-toe in black, pushing me on a swing—my unexceptional style consisting of an oversized sweatshirt, jeans, sandals, and long dark hair rippling out behind me like a mass of ribbons. I ran my fingers through my now short hair, lighter than darker these days with increasing greyness, trying to remember the last time I had long hair. Teddie was standing next to us in the photo, short and plump and attired in ordinary, no-nonsense clothes, her kinky-haired head bent low as she laughed wildly at something one of us must have just said.

Another shot was a close-up of Grace, sticking her tongue out and crossing her eyes and holding up her middle finger, her long blond hair in its usual unkempt, stringy condition. And Rachel in all her understated elegance, a sweater over a turtleneck with corduroys, stretched out on our couch, her dazzling smile beaming at the camera just above the top edges of a book. *I bet she still wears turtlenecks and corduroys and sweaters.* And a picture of Julie and me, lying together in a hammock, the quintessential image of happily-ever-after, taken shortly before she destroyed that myth.

These were the best friends of my youth, the women with whom I had lived during our junior and senior years of college, the women with whom I pledged undying allegiance, never believing, all those many years ago, that we wouldn't always stay as close as we were in yet one more picture: graduation day—the six of us laughing uproariously, our mortarboards tumbling in the air above our heads, twined arms connecting us, leaning into our love for one another. It would be good to see these women again. Even Julie.

I glanced back at the invitation. June would be perfect for me, as I intended to leave for Minnesota that month, to spend the summer with Mary Sharon and her sweetie, Celia. I could drive to Seattle, and Mary Sharon could fly there, the two of us driving back to Minnesota together. *It would be swell,* I thought, *to spend some time alone with Mary Sharon.* Celia was a dear, but Mary Sharon and I never got to spend any time by ourselves since the two of them had become a couple. *Maybe we could drive back to Minnesota through Canada.* I decided I'd better call Mary Sharon to see what she thought. I picked the obit up, idly wondering why Rachel would send it. It's not as if I had ever known Grace's father or even knew Grace anymore.

Rich Stone, Local Real Estate Developer

Richard A. Stone died at home on March 6, 1995, surrounded by his wife and children and grandchildren, following a valiant battle with heart disease.

Rich Stone was born in Minneapolis in 1929 to Charles and Lillian Stone, attended Roosevelt High School and the University of Minnesota. Besides loving his work, he was an avid skier and golfer. Rich was prominent in many social service organizations and an active member of St. Paul's Episcopal Church of Edina. He sang in the choir and was involved in church administration. In addition, he served on the board of the Harriet Tubman Women's Shelter and a number of other professional boards.

Stone had a great vision for land development. He started Stone Development in 1955 and built it to a well-respected corporation in subsequent years. He created and developed A Stone's Throw, the innovative and eco-sound planned community just south of the Minnesota River. He was the instigator and main mover of The Stonewall Project, affordable housing in the inner city. Many other building projects in the Twin Cities, residential and business, have the Stone Development mark on them.

He was preceded in death by his parents and two siblings, Doris Stone Marshall and Charles Stone, Jr. Besides his wife, Evangelina, he is survived by a son, Richard A. Stone, Jr., of Wayzata; two daughters, Hope Stone Winston of Kansas City, Missouri, and Grace Stone of Seattle, Washington; and six grandchildren. A memorial service will be held at 1 p.m. at St. Paul's Episcopal Church of Edina. In lieu of flowers, memorial donations to Harriet Tubman Women's Shelter or the False Memory Syndrome Foundation of Philadelphia would be appreciated.

"What!?" I shouted aloud, causing my golden retriever, Agatha Christie, generally known as Aggie, to rouse herself and stare intently at me. She was twelve now and startled easily. "Sorry, Girl," I mumbled, reaching down to ruffle the fur on her head. "This is just so astounding!"

I glanced at the clock on my desk. Two p.m. I closed my eyes a minute. That meant—what?—four o'clock in Minnesota. I could probably still get Mary Sharon at work. I picked up the phone and dialed her number. *The False Memory Syndrome Foundation,* I thought. *Now it's showing up in people's requests for memorial donations?* The phone was ringing. *It means, almost certainly, that one of his children or all of them accused him of raping them or molesting them or abusing them, in some way.* It gave me the creeps. There was little doubt in my mind: one of the kids in the Stone family *had been* abused. Of course, this didn't entirely surprise me, as we'd kind of suspected way back in college, there was "something funny" about Grace's family. She was such an odd bird herself, plus she never let us go home with her.

"Nice hours, Mary Sharon," I murmured as I hung up and dialed her home number. She and Celia lived in my grandmother's house in Stony River, a few miles from Grand Marais, Minnesota. I'd inherited it from my mother when she died and renovated it a few years ago; however, I wasn't yet ready to leave my hometown of San Francisco—although on particularly bad days of smog, traffic clog, and rude clerks, I thought I must be crazy. Mary Sharon and Celia had tranformed the house into a B & B. It was big enough to allow me to spend the summer there without affecting their business. "Gone fishing," her message machine informed me. "Call later or leave a message. We'll get back to you."

"Mary Sharon," I intoned after the beep, "call me right away. Have you gotten an invite from Rachel yet? Did she include Grace's father's obit in it? Call me! Fishing? When did you start that? Honest to god, I can't quite imagine you in a boat with worms or something. What do you *wear* fishing? Call me!"

I hung up, a grin replacing the scowl on my face. Fishing. Mary Sharon's inimitable style—the black of her youth succeeded by a cacophony of bold colors usually clashing with one another, odd materials, draping, flowing shapes, and wide sashes—truly did not lend itself to the image of baiting hooks or snapping motor ropes or rowing. Fishing? It was good it was almost June now, and I'd be heading to Minnesota soon to see for myself what changes had been wrought. It had been Celia's voice on the machine. Maybe she was the one who went fishing. That I could imagine. Celia could easily blend in with that bunch of hearty northwoods women on the North Shore of Lake Superior. But Mary Sharon? Naaah.

As Aggie and I drove north from San Francisco two weeks later, I let my mind drift back to my college days. I had chosen to drive up Highway 1, something I hadn't done for years, giving myself plenty of time to dawdle. I enjoyed the incredible vistas that stretched mile after mile along this oceanside highway, mostly unsettled, rugged land. Rachel had agreed to Aggie's presence at our reunion, the only outsider, because I'd be going to Minnesota after the gathering, and Aggie, of course, would be going with me.

It was 1971 when I had headed for the University of Minnesota. My parents had been surprised. After all, I grew up in San Francisco. I was rebellious and a little wild, and they had assumed I would want to go to one of the many colleges in the Bay

Area with notoriously radical reputations—San Francisco State or Santa Cruz or Berkeley. What they didn't know, however, was that I'd already had a fling with another girl in high school and needed to get far away from home to properly explore this unknown territory. Also, their battles, heretofore remaining underground, were beginning to erupt with regularity, and I wanted to be out of the line of their fire.

I had a strong attachment to Minnesota because my mother, for the first thirteen years of my life, took my sister, Magdalene, and me there every summer to visit our grandparents. The University of Minnesota, at that time, also boasted about its journalism department, considered one of the top ten in the country. I knew I was going to major in journalism, so Minnesota it was. A place where I was mostly unknown, a place far away, and still a place with roots.

Those of us starting college in the early '70s were products of the flower children culture that had spread across the country during the '60s. The raucous and relentless beat and the call-to-arms lyrics of the Beatles and the Grateful Dead and the Rolling Stones pulsed through our veins while the gentler and more thoughtful words and sounds of Joan Baez and Bob Dylan and Joni Mitchell informed our worldview. Our icons and heroes, too often, were young, dead, druggie rock stars such as Jim Morrison, Janis Joplin, and Jimi Hendrix. We read Germaine Greer and James Baldwin and Harper Lee, Simone de Beauvoir and Ken Kesey and Angela Davis. Many of us knew boys who'd died in Vietnam while others knew boys who were in prison or had fled to Canada. Even though the 'Nam War and the Evers, King, and Kennedy assassinations as well as police brutality had left scars on our souls, we still believed in the revolutionary possibilities of the '60s, still believed things were going to change. And we believed that *we* were going to be the ones to change them. We were also beginning to understand and embrace feminism, although our skirts barely reached below our asses and our hair hung nearly as low.

Well. *My* skirts were not miniskirts. Actually, *my* skirts were pants. I was a large girl, nearly six feet, with a full body that recalled the Vikings in my distant past and a plainness to my features that was common among people of mixed descent from northern and middle European countries. I had no desire to call more attention to myself, so I lived in bell-bottomed jeans and sweatshirts and loose Mexican shirts.

Of course, I was registered to live in a dorm. No self-respecting "political" girl would think of joining a sorority in 1971. I vividly recall walking into my Comstock Dormitory room that first day.

"Wow!" an incredibly odd-looking girl said. "You must be from Iceland. You're so tall!" She strode across the minuscule space in this miniature room with her hand outstretched, "Hi! I'm Mary Sharon Andrews, from Rocky Ridge, Minnesota. Where are you from?"

"*You're* from Minnesota?" I responded, in what I was later to learn was a not uncommon California provincialism. This Mary Sharon didn't fit any of the stereotypes *I* had of what a Minnesotan would look like. She was a hybrid, I guess, of beatnik, hippie, and heavy metal rocker—a category barely conceptualized at that time, resulting from Steppenwolf's use of William Burroughs' phrase, "heavy metal thunder." Her hair was the color of black that you knew was dyed: too-black and too-flat and too-lifeless. It hung to her waist in back but on top was cut short in varying heights, looking a bit as if someone had just pulled hunks out, leaving other hunks in a random pattern across the top of her head.

I spoke before thinking. "Did you do your hair with a wire cutter or something?" I then grabbed her hand, a little afraid of having her for a roommate but also afraid of totally alienating her.

She laughed. "That's a good one. A wire cutter! I'll have to try that next time. No. I used my mom's pinking shears."

"You did?" I was still staring. "Why?"

She laughed again. "I dunno. Just wanted to see how it would look, I guess. Boy, you're direct, aren't you?" But she was smiling, so I didn't feel like she was pissed off or anything.

I smiled back, trying to cover my sudden attack of shyness. "Yeah, I guess I am. Or maybe just stupid." This time we both laughed. "I'm Tyler Jones. I'm from San Francisco. I'm Norwegian and German on my mother's side and mostly German, with some Hungarian, on my father's side. I guess Icelandic and Norwegian come from common stock, though. How come you guessed that? No one has ever identified me as Scandinavian before." For one thing, I wasn't blond—which I suspected she was, under all that dye—and my eyes were a watery blue-green or green-blue, depending on what I was wearing, rather than the vivid Minnesota-lakes blue her eyes were.

"This little town I grew up in? Wasn't far from a mostly Icelandic settlement. They were big. Bigger than all the other Scandinavians living out there on the plains. I'm Norwegian, myself, and German, too. So we're probably sisters, of a sort."

I thought this whole conversation was exceedingly odd. I had no recollection, in my previous eighteen years, of ever having had a discussion about ancestry at all. "What's your sign?" was the most common question Californians asked about one's heritage. Of course, whenever I came to Minnesota, friends and relatives all fussed about how I looked like "this one" or "that one." But in California? Never.

And we *were* like sisters, or at least like you might imagine sisters to be. *My* sister and I were certainly never close like Mary Sharon and I were, especially because Magdalene and I were on opposite ends of the good/bad spectrum. It wasn't that I was so bad, really, it's just that *in comparison to her,* I seemed bad. Whereas she was quiet and well-behaved, I was—according to my mother—"mouthy, inquisitive, rebellious, and annoyingly energetic." While I dreamed of being a hippie during my growing-up years, Magdalene emulated Loretta Young or Audrey Hepburn or Jacqueline Kennedy. Of course, she could aspire to that standard, being much smaller than my Amazonian proportions.

Sometimes I wondered if we would have been different if we had been born into each other's bodies. What would I have been like if I'd been 5'5", weighed 120 pounds, had hair the color of sunlit-dipped strawberries and eyes the color of icy-blue fjords? And what would Magda have been like if she'd been almost six feet tall, weighed 200-plus pounds, had hair the color of a dusty gravel road and eyes the color of 1930s blue-green linoleum? Did any of that make a difference? Probably. And still, the fact is, I wouldn't trade places with Magdalene, who now lives in southern California and is gracious hostess to her husband's important business colleagues, harried carpooler to her children's busy lives, proper churchgoer, and polite denier of her pervert sister's life.

But plenty of times while I was growing up, I wished I had her body instead of mine. *How was it,* I would moan, *that Magda got the eyes and hair of a lovely Scandinavian maiden, and I got the hulking body of a Viking warrior?* Once, when I was groaning about all of this to Mary Sharon, she replied, "Because you can."

"What?"

"Because you can," she repeated. "You *can* be full bodied, you *can* be tall, you *can* have fabulous presence, you *can* carry yourself like a royal emissary. *You* can make your mark in the world, even change it. And all Magda can do is be someone's server, someone's caretaker, someone's decorative object."

I looked askance at her. "You're saying . . . This is pretty metaphysical, Mary Sharon. You think that who you are capable of being in the world is predetermined and, consequently, determines your body and your looks?"

"Sure. Why not?"

"But don't you think it's the other way around? You're fat, so you're *not* a tennis pro. You're thin, so you're *not* an opera singer. You're thin, so you *are* a ballet dancer. You're fat, so you are . . . what? What do fat people get to be? . . . a department store Santa Claus? Don't you think?"

"Oh, no," she disagreed, and we were off and running, sometimes all night—talking, weighing our ideas, analyzing, holding thoughts up to the light, examining, falling into bed too exhausted to get up for classes, and still getting up. It was like this for the four years we were at college together. It's still like this, twenty years later. No subject is ever too trivial for us to dismiss, too large for us to tackle.

Even more astonishing to us, even though we often took opposite viewpoints to thoroughly scrutinize a subject, we—more often than not—were in perfect agreement with each other. Now, after all these years, we talk in a kind of shorthand, so developed are our communication abilities. I can start a sentence and have no problem with Mary Sharon finishing it, and vice versa. Neither of us has ever had a romantic relationship that approximated our friendship. This is another subject we scrutinize.

"You've had more romances than I have," Mary Sharon once said recently, "so what do you think, with all your experience?"

"I don't know if it works that way, Mary Sharon. My relationships average about one year each, while your two major relationships have lasted ten years and five years. I think that probably qualifies *you* to be the expert. Not me."

"Okay. This is what I think: friendships are the healthiest relationships most of us have. When it comes to friends, we're attracted to people *like* us. Too often, it seems to me, when it comes to 'love,' we're attracted to people who are—what?"

"Is this a test? How about: we're attracted to people who are most like the people we couldn't get along with in our family?" I said this as if it were the first time I'd uttered such a thought, instead of the more likely seven-hundredth time.

"Bingo!"

"I'm not going to argue with you, although I'd like to point out that I think you do this a lot less than I do, which is why *my* relationships are so brief. I also think that maybe the kind of passion you and I have for each other—and this goes for any good friends—might get ruined if we tried to force it into a 'love' thing."

She agreed by nodding, and I knew we were both thinking about the one time we'd made love. We didn't repeat it. "But Tyler, maybe you give up too soon. Ever think of that?"

"Well, dear friend, if I hadn't, you would've reminded me. After all, every time I become single again, you bring this up."

"Really, Tyler, Julie was the longest relationship you ever had, wasn't she? What was that? Four years? And that was twenty years ago!"

"Five," I correct her. "We were together *five* years. And it was seventeen years ago. And, lest we get lost here in an examination of my relationships or lack thereof, could I also remind you that I lost a few years to drinking?"

"What a handy excuse," she always exclaimed at this point.

Five years. Now I was forty-two years old, and the longest relationship I'd ever had lasted five years and was seventeen years ago. Not counting my therapist, that is. Did that make me a failure?

But Julie was not the next to enter our orbit, anyway. For most of that first year, Mary Sharon and I were inseparable. We took and cut the same classes, we demonstrated against the war that was finally winding down, we joined American Indian Movement demonstrations, we went to lectures, concerts, movies, coffeehouses together, talking the sun up more mornings than not. We were quite a sight—Mary Sharon with her look-at-me hairdos and mismatched, cast-off wardrobe, entirely black, and me with my toned-down, ordinary, don't-look-at-me style. What people must have thought! Of course, if I really didn't want anyone to notice me, would I have been hanging out with a Mary Sharon? I don't think so. I guess I just didn't want to garner the attention directly, but—at the same time—I didn't want to be lost altogether. No chance of that.

Many of our professors started dreading our presence. We often wouldn't sit near each other but would start a sort of tag-team approach to questioning, prodding, challenging our teachers.

"Professor Ott? Do you think we can really analyze the meaning of 'The Rape of Lucrece' without examining what rape means in a complicit society?" Mary Sharon might say.

And before he could really recover from such an astonishing question, I might put my oar in and say, "And while we're at it, Professor Ott, could you tell me why none of our texts are by women this quarter? Or blacks? Or anyone but dead white men?"

We were both devouring the feminist books that were beginning to pop up everywhere and bringing "impertinent or irrelevant" questions to the classroom. Other students adored us or hated us, and we didn't much care, either way. We were having the time of our lives. For a while, we fancied we were in love but soon decided we were soul mates instead. Mary Sharon was already sure of and committed to loving women while I wavered, going out with boys frequently but getting crushes even more frequently on girls and my few women teachers.

In the spring of that first year, we took a class on Women in Revolutionary Movements, taught by a feminist in the History Department. We had almost no opportunity to trot out our "dog-and-pony show" because this class left little for us to criticize or confront. We were enthralled by the information we were gathering about women all over the world—in China, Russia, Cuba—resisting the status quo.

In that class was a short, pudgy, kinky-haired girl with toffee-colored skin. She was the other reason we didn't do our usual obstructionist show: she was even more vociferous in her challenges than the two of us. She was a fiery dissenter and passionate orator. She knew things neither of us knew and wasn't afraid to say or ask anything. We were a little in awe of her; we wanted to know her better; actually, we wanted to *be* her.

We were unnaturally shy, however. Although Mary Sharon and I had both been involved in civil rights during our high school years, neither of us had ever had any black kids as friends. Mary Sharon had grown up in an all-white small town in western Minnesota. I had insisted on going to a racially mixed public school in San Francisco although my sister Magdalene had gone to private school. I mingled and worked with kids of all races and backgrounds in student demonstrations and city wide protests for students' rights, civil rights, and against state-sanctioned police and military violence. Even so, my friends were white. Black kids, or others, never invited me home with them. And I didn't invite them home with me.

So we wanted to be friends with Theodora Bannon but didn't know how to approach her. After all, this was the end of a decade of black organizing in which many blacks were emphasizing racial purity and separatism. And then there was the problem of color itself. We weren't, exactly, certain that she *was* black. I mean, she was clearly a mixture of some sort because her dark skin was on the light side. And what if she wasn't black at all but just a dark Italian or something? It could be. We were so terrified of looking like we wanted to be friends *because* she was black instead of because she was clearly a brilliant feminist that we did nothing; we were paralyzed into inaction.

Then one day in class, it was all settled. Theodora was raving about how women, who'd been in the midst of decision making and on the front lines, were expected to go back home and start birthing new "revolutionaries"—that would be boys—and female children to service those revolutionaries once the revolutions were successful. She was livid and was making an analogy to black activist men whose attitudes were the same toward black activist women, saying, "All this talk of 'unity' with our men! Where are they on *our* issues?"

We were caught up in her fervor, and Mary Sharon quoted from Florynce Kennedy, a black attorney who was going about the country, lecturing on feminism. "Unity in a movement situation is overrated. If you were the Establishment, which would you rather see coming in the door, five hundred mice or one lion?"

And while the class was still puzzling that out, I quoted from *The Dialectic of Sex* by Shulamith Firestone, ". . . black men would eventually want what all men want: to be on top of their women." A lively and angry debate broke out as to women's destiny and true usefulness and the concept of men and women as equals.

After class, Teddie (as we would soon be calling her) asked us if we wanted to go for a Coke or something. "Yes!" we answered exuberantly and simultaneously, as if we were Siamese twins or something, then lapsed into tongue-tied embarrassment at our too-obvious eagerness.

But Teddie chuckled and said, "I guess I didn't have to be so shy about asking you sooner."

We immediately shed our mortification, only to cloak ourselves in it again by falling all over each other, physically and linguistically, in our ardent keenness to impress her. Eventually, we settled down enough to actually make ourselves coherent and at least passably likeable. It turned out that Teddie, too, had had her eye on us for awhile, feeling quite certain that we would be intellectual equals and, probably, friends.

"Are you a couple?" she asked, which shocked us that first day at Coffman, the student union. No one talked openly about being a lesbian in those days. At least no one we knew.

We both laughed, and I said, "In a way. Except probably not like you mean. A couple of what, do you think?" I directed this statement toward Mary Sharon.

"A couple of nuts, maybe?" she finished. "A couple of soul mates, I guess. But not a romantic couple, assuming that's what you meant." Teddie nodded. "I *am* a lesbian," Mary Sharon announced, "and she's more or less undecided." She waved a hand at me, and I realized I felt none of my usual annoyance at her bluntness. "But we're not in love with each other. Not like that, anyway."

Teddie nodded solemnly and said, "As for me, I love men, but I'm a dedicated feminist. Which sometimes means there aren't too many men I like."

We dissolved into laughter, beginning the bonding process. And Teddie promptly abandoned men anyway, at least in bed, when she met Rachel and fell, as the saying goes, head over heels.

It was the beginning of our sophomore year. Teddie had gone home to Boston for the summer and brought us a wonderful gift when she returned: a pamphlet, *Our Bodies, Ourselves,* created by a group calling itself the Boston Women's Health Book Collective. We were lying on the grass of the college quad, reading it aloud to one another, and wondering at its frank details and honesty about women's bodies. We were also talking about the possibility of a Women's Studies Department. We had all joined University Women's Liberation the year before. Mary Sharon and I had already been to a meeting this year and were describing to Teddie the task force the committee had just created to develop a curriculum that would place women at the center. Teddie was eager to get involved, too.

I had also gone home for the summer, to a part-time job in a bookstore in San Francisco and avoidance of my parents' house. Mary Sharon was the only one of us who'd stayed in Minneapolis, getting a room in one of the many boarding houses in a commercial area bordering the campus called Dinkytown. She worked in a coffeehouse nights and a laundromat during the day. Her partial scholarship didn't cover all her expenses, and her parents couldn't help her much with the rest, so she had to earn as much money as she could.

We were all feeling good that day because we'd landed part-time campus jobs. Mary Sharon and I at the student union, waiting tables—Mary Sharon because she had to and me because I wanted spending money that I didn't have to ask for. Teddie was so brilliant that she was on a full academic scholarship, but—like me—she wanted some independence, so she had just gotten a job in the administration offices.

We were full of high spirits and babbling with delight at reuniting with one another and what we perceived to be a meaningful life. Suddenly, we saw her at the same time, stopped talking, and—I swear—we all fell a little in love at that moment. Of course, the only one who acted on that ridiculous reaction, the only one with enough chutzpah, was Teddie, who jumped to her feet and trotted over to this stunning girl.

"Hi! I'm Theadora Bannon. Are you new here?"—an absurd question, because the U was so large, we could've gone to school for four years without having seen many of the students.

"Rachel Fineberg," came the answer, and we sighed a collective sigh of relief that she hadn't brushed Teddie off. By then, Mary Sharon and I had managed to get to our feet, too, and introduced ourselves as well.

How do I describe Rachel? She seemed to move as if she weren't actually lifting one foot after another. She was neither thin nor fat, just in-between, but she had a posture that was so imposing that it literally screamed "pride." I was always able to pick her out, even in a large crowd, by that dignified, composed posture.

Although I started the long process of becoming more comfortable with my body in college, I was still self-conscious about my size, resulting in my having the presence of something akin to an awkward bear. Mary Sharon, a willowy 5'7", mostly disguised her body in layers of black. Although she certainly had a lot of presence, it was mostly perceived as wacky. And Teddie's rounded petiteness often undercut her ardent opinions. If she'd been white, blond, and blue-eyed, she'd have been pegged as a cheerleader.

While the three of us were all making some kind of statement with the adorning of our bodies, Rachel was simply and effortlessly elegant, even though she was wearing, that day, jeans with a cotton shirt and a tweed vest. Her black hair was cropped closely to her well-formed head, but one could see that the short strands longed to loop into curls. The flecks of gold in her brown-sugar colored eyes glinted with mirth, I think, at our puppy-dog-like eagerness to meet her. The thing about Rachel that attracted everyone, the thing that was absolutely matchless, was that she exuded confidence, both in her physical presence and in her articulation. In some way that we didn't even know or recognize yet, we all longed for that confidence.

Later, I was to realize that some of Rachel's presence was surface; she knew how to appear supremely at ease even when she wasn't. And the rest of it was the result of a combination of secure money in her background, parents who loved her almost unconditionally, especially because she was the only one upon whom they had to shower this adoration, and years of dance training. She was from "old money": lumber on her mother's side and imports/exports on her father's side. She grew up in one of the stately mansions on Summit Avenue in St. Paul, but—aside from that—neither of her parents were exactly following family traditions. Her mother was a college professor, and her father was a union organizer. Both were fiery politicos. Lucky for us, because it would have been awkward if we'd gone charging after this girl's affection and attention and then had discovered she didn't share our values or passionate politics. With her parents and background, she made us look like naifs.

We were all jealous, having no idea that anyone's parents could be like Rachel's. My mother, actually, was on the brink of becoming a committed Peace and Justice Movement radical, but I didn't know that then and couldn't even have imagined it. Oh, I knew she was getting involved in political actions that disturbed my conservative banker father, but I just thought she was rebelling against him. My parents were dull and proper: all-too-predictable, upper-middle-class Republicans.

And Mary Sharon's parents were nice people who were working-class Democrats but weren't particularly interested in politics. Her father worked in the farmers' co-op, and her mother was a homemaker. Both of Teddie's parents were schoolteachers, both cautious people. As she put it, they supported the Civil Rights Movement and were appalled by the problems in Boston over desegregation. They, nonetheless, stayed safely on the sidelines and encouraged their children to do the same. Their one incautious act, marrying each other—she was white, he was black—seemed to be enough for them.

But Rachel had grown up on picket lines, on sit-ins and sit-downs, in marches and protests. Her parents had been involved in voter registration and freedom marches in scary places like Mississippi and Louisiana and Alabama, where white northern "do-gooder-busybodies" were targeted for harassment, even murder, by hostile white southerners. She had gone along on some of these actions, been left with appalled grandparents on others. When the Vietnam War came along, peace demonstrations, flag burnings, massive draft-resistance rallies, and riots were added to her family's agenda. Rachel regaled us with stories for hours on end. We all vied to go home with her and hang out with her parents at every opportunity we got. She was both amused and annoyed by this.

"I like to think you are friends with me because I'm *me,* not because I have these fascinating parents," she'd acidly state. She was proud and fond of her parents, but as she continually pointed out to us, "They *are* just parents, you know. Sometimes they bug me, like anyone's parents."

We agreed politely but didn't *really* believe her. What we believed was that she *wanted* to be like other kids, *wanted* to complain about her parents, even though her parents gave her little reason to do so. And we, good friends that we were, tried to be sympathetic with her because she clearly needed that from us. But secretly? We believed her parents and her home life were idyllic.

With Rachel, we also got Grace Stone. At first, the rest of us weren't sure we liked Grace. She was the textbook hippie: blond hair hanging lankly below her shoulders and parted in the middle; battered jeans with tattered hems covering dirty feet, which were usually bare; raggedy t-shirts; and the lackluster eyes that accompanied most regular pot users.

We *all* did some pot smoking. And we'd tried other drugs— especially acid and speed—at some time or other. But, now that we were about the serious work of change, our use was negligible. We couldn't be hampered with that stuff. We were rather self-righteously proud of our relative purity. Of course, we didn't even count drinking, and none of us drank very much anyway. Then.

"Give her a chance," Rachel insisted. "She's had a hard time of it, but underneath is a heart of gold. And she's funny! Believe me, I've known her forever."

We were puzzled. Rachel was clearly like us, committed to fomenting social change, while Grace just seemed committed to annoying her wealthy, conventional parents. Her father was some kind of builder, and her mother was a professional volunteer—or so Rachel told us. None of us were ever invited home with Grace to Edina, a wealthy Minneapolis suburb, nor did any of us want to be. Actually, we weren't certain she ever went home herself. She didn't talk about her parents at all, except with an occasional sneer.

But Rachel was right. In spite of Grace's almost constant moroseness, she was wickedly funny, especially good at making us laugh at our overly serious selves. And she was compassionate, tender even, in the most surprising and necessary times. Nonetheless, we never truly felt we knew her. It was as if she were always on the periphery of our group, agreeing with us politically, but seldom actually participating in any obvious way. Mostly, it seemed like Grace was barely present in our lives.

I thought about the Grace-I-barely-knew and her father's obituary and the False Memory Syndrome Foundation. Those who created and rely heavily on the Foundation often do not want to take responsibility for the abuse in their families and/or do not want to believe it happened. And, of course, in some few cases it didn't happen. Mostly, they believe that the accuser has been coerced or convinced, falsely, by a therapist that childhood abuse occurred. Some believe that the accuser simply made up the abuse story to get attention. Sometimes these things do happen. And those occasional falsehoods cast unfortunate doubt on the vast majority of truthful accusations.

Those of us who work against violence-against-women weigh in on the side of believing victims' stories, simply because they are usually true. And when I thought of Grace during our college years—her pot smoking, extreme moodiness, frequent disappearances, and insistence on her asexuality—and put that together with what I know now about classic abuse symptoms, it made perfect sense to me that she was the victim of some kind of abuse.

We learned to love what we could of her and just accept the rest, lowering our expectations for her. She was, in our own vernacular, "just Grace." None of us ever got close to her; actually, she never *let* any of us close to her. Except Rachel, whose relationship with Grace was almost secretive, shutting the rest of us out, even Teddie. Rachel was very protective of Grace, supporting her when the rest of us were annoyed by her odd comings and goings, her withdrawn manner, her sulky countenance.

We spent countless hours that year, with other students and eventually with teachers, working with the Task Force on Women's Studies. We were a force to reckon with, the four of us, Teddie and Rachel and Mary Sharon and me, organizing events with others on campus that dramatized the gender disparity both in our educational system and in the larger society, leading discussions in and out of classrooms, pushing all the departments to include more women in their curriculum and staff. We finally had a core of professors, those early women's studies teachers, who appreciated us. By the end of the year, we knew we would actually have a "department of our own" the following year.

Teddie and Rachel became a couple, Teddie quickly shedding her heterosexuality in favor of Rachel's superior attractions. Mary Sharon continued "dating." We called her the campus slut, which quickly became, amongst ourselves only, Mary Sharon Shlut, and we laughed gleefully at our daring.

And Grace simply shook her head and said, "Not me. No women or men. I'm asexual." Mary Sharon insisted that just meant she was waiting for the right woman to come along. Grace would shake her head again, "Shame on you, Mary Sharon! That's like saying 'you just need a good lay.' Believe it or not, you don't know everything. Me—I'm saving myself for me. That's it."

I was still dating the occasional boy, insisting that if I couldn't have Rachel or Teddie, I might as well date men. Of course, this was all before Julie came on the scene.

I didn't like Julie. None of us did. It was winter quarter, our sophomore year. All five of us were taking a course called American Women Writers. It was taught by a white woman in the English Department and had only white women writers in the syllabus. It was a wonderful class with fabulous reading assignments, but we were disappointed that this professor, an obvious feminist, was reproducing the white elitism so prevalent throughout the university system. We let our displeasure be known at the first class, our collective politic shining, we thought, in its purity and integrity.

A woman none of us knew raised her hand and disagreed with us. "I understand the sentiment expressed here," she said in clear, measured tones, and I thought then that I couldn't stand her, she was so devoid of passion, "but I would like to put forth another point of view. Although I certainly agree that it would be best to have a class like this be more representative of our entire American society, are we willing, nonetheless, to throw the baby out with the bathwater? It doesn't take much scrutiny of the present CLA catalog to discern how little is being done in *any* department that focuses on women. We are, after all, being exposed to some of the finest women writers in this course. And, it seems to me, it behooves us to remember who our enemies are."

She stunned us to silence with her audacity to question our radical credentials. "Thank you, Julie," the professor responded, and I thought—*a brown-noser.* My lip curled a little, wondering what this clearly inappropriate person was doing in this class. She looked like a sorority girl with her makeup, carefully coifed, medium-length, brown hair, pleated skirt, and sweater set. A *1950s* sorority girl at that.

Afterward, we all buzzed with one another about this Julie. "We-should-remember-who-our-enemies-are," Teddie mimicked her.

"The height of arrogance!" intoned Rachel. "Thinking it's necessary to educate *us*! And you want to ask her if she thinks black women and other nonwhite women think it's better to have any class that focusses on women, even if it's only white women."

"Humphh," Grace agreed, her mouth full of candy bar.

"Oh, I don't know," Mary Sharon said, and we all looked at her in astonishment. "Don't you think it might be just a *little* arrogant of us to assume we don't need any educating?" We continued to stare at her. "Anyway, I thought she was kinda cute."

"Oh, Mary Sharon Shlut," I groaned. "I swear, you're as bad as any guy. Do you always just think with your clit?" We howled at my audacity, using a word aloud none of us had ever heard *or* read until we started talking to each other and reading *Our Bodies,*

Ourselves. "You don't *really* think she's cute, do you? I mean, look at her clothes! I'm sure that hairdo requires hair spray. She looks like she's in the wrong decade!"

Mary Sharon just smiled and nudged me with her black ballet-slippered foot. "Don't be such a snob, Tyler."

Of course, in the end, it was me who thought she was "kinda cute." The way we got together was so classic, so typical of anyone growing up digesting Hollywood's version of love, it's almost embarrassing. We spent the entire quarter sparring with one another, taking opposite stands on almost every issue that arose. She was smart, I'd give her that, it's just that she was so *moderate*—always wanting to placate rather than rattle others' consciousness, believing that education could accomplish more than overthrow. Gradually, although I didn't notice it at first, none of the rest of my group were arguing with Julie. It somehow became this "thing" between her and me: sparks flying while we both dug in, oblivious to what others were beginning to discern.

My friends began to drop hints. "Have you noticed that Julie Patterson's style has started to change?" Rachel innocently observed one day.

"What change?" I snarled. "She's just as cold and 'reasonable' as ever."

"I didn't mean her oratory style, Tyler," Rachel murmured.

I scowled, and Grace said, "Yeah. I can't remember the last time she wore a skirt. And the makeup and hair spray seem to have disappeared, too. Pouf! Out the window."

"Well, you know," Mary Sharon said in that slow, backcountry intonation she donned at times, "it's my theory that Julie just needed to see how other girls were dressing to start figuring out what she wanted for herself. After all, she comes from a farm, and you know how those rural folk are." She drawled the words "rural folk" out. "Don't know much about big-city style. I mean, really! Look at me!" She was wearing faded black tights with a heavily balled black sweater reaching almost to her knees and her usual black ballet slippers, although she had stitched silver sequins all over them. Her fingernails, as usual, were painted black to match her lipstick and hair. "It's obvious, isn't it, that I don't know a *thing* about how to dress properly! It's what you'd expect from a small town girl, you betcha."

We all laughed, then laughed some more when Grace said, "Yeah, I'll bet you were homecoming queen out there at Rocky Ridge High, weren't you, Shlut?"

When we stopped laughing, I asked Mary Sharon, "How do you know she's from a farm?"

She arched an eyebrow at me before answering. "Caught that, did you? Because I ran into her one day at the union, and we had a Coke."

And that's when I first began to think I might be interested in Julie, although I was still trying to deny it, because I felt a twinge of jealousy. At the end of the quarter, Julie asked me if I "wanted to go for a Coke," and within a week, I was no longer going out with guys.

It was fire and ice, good and bad, sweet and sour from the beginning: we were convinced that we complemented each other. We certainly honed our persuasive abilities by constant analysis and argumentation—both of us on the same side but voicing our concerns and beliefs in different ways. It was exhilarating, in and out of bed. Years later, when I heard the concept, "Lesbians are the only people who yell at one another while actually agreeing," I always thought of Julie and me. Julie, who could create an instant bonfire in my gut just by touching my arm, and Julie, who could just as instantly wither my desire by a condescending remark. Julie, whose love of books equalled mine, and Julie, who had never heard of Art Tatum or Billie Holiday or Satchmo but who soon loved jazz as totally as I did while introducing me to Bach, Mozart, Handel,

Beethoven. And Julie, who was—in spite of her sometimes reluctant activism—the creative force behind many of our actions.

None of us went home that summer between our sophomore and junior years. Instead, we rented a flat in an old converted mansion, not far from campus. There were two bedrooms, a sunroom that was supposed to pass as a living room, and a kitchen. The kitchen was enormous, so we made it our combination kitchen/living room. Rachel and Teddie got one bedroom, Julie and I got the other one, and Mary Sharon and Grace got the sunroom.

"Oh, great," Grace complained. "I live with a bunch of dykes, not to speak of the fact that my roommate is the biggest slut on campus. What is everyone going to think of me?"

"That you're cool!" we all shouted in unison.

"Sure," she harrumphed. "What they're gonna think is that Mary Sharon and I are an item!"

"You could do worse, Grace," Mary Sharon retorted.

"Sweetie," Grace shot back, "I *have* done worse."

"What I want to know," Mary Sharon asked, "is how come Grace and I just automatically ended up with the sunroom? I mean, don't any of you want it? Shouldn't we draw straws or something?"

Teddie giggled. "We're *couples,* Mary Sharon. We can't be bedding down in that fishbowl."

"Plus there's no door," I added. "The rest of us need doors."

Mary Sharon frowned. "What if I want to bring someone home?"

"You can't bring someone home!" Grace shouted. "That's my bedroom, too." The rest of us started to fade away, hoping to leave them to work it out between themselves. "Oh, no you don't!"

Grace shouted again. "Get back in here. We have a lot of house rules to work out!"

And we did, with excessive laughter, a fair amount of grumpiness, and much love. We created a rotating schedule for kitchen and bathroom cleanup and cooking. Everything else we simply took care of individually. In terms of finances, we pooled our money according to an income-averaging system, so that those of us with more money paid, proportionately, for more of our expenses. We thought we were brilliant, forging new paths of collective living.

Eventually, Mary Sharon took care of the lack of a door by creating her own version of a beaded doorway. Combining her feminism and woman-identification with her artistic leanings, Mary Sharon dipped tampons in black paint and rolled them in glitter, then glued them together to hang in ribbons in the doorway. Grace pretended scorn, but the rest of us simply adored the innovation.

These were the friends I was driving to see, the friends of my youth, the women who probably did more to shape my future than even my family. We thought, back then, that we would always be in one another's lives. I guess most college pals assume that. But when Julie left me, she severed her ties to all of us. Grace moved to Seattle after graduation, although I found that out from Rachel because Grace herself made no farewells to the rest of us. I went back to San Francisco after Julie left me, and Teddie moved to Washington, D.C. Rachel and Mary Sharon remained in Minnesota. It would be good to bring our lives together again, to catch up with one another.

Reliving the jumble of events and relationships that marked my college years, I made my way to Seattle. My reverie was frequently interrupted by my own gasps as I traveled up that most serpentine and scenic of roads: California's infamous Highway 1. It dipped in and out of valleys, shimmied through small towns, hugged the cliffs of the coastal mountains—making my hands damp with perspiration as I crept along the precipitous edge of this continent, sharp walls of rock plummeting hundreds of feet to pounding surf throwing itself against the tumbled scree at the foot of these craggy mammoths. Relentless sun and the heaving mass of the Pacific, shimmering with the dazzle of light on water, and the dizzying precipices were, indeed, distracting.

In Oregon, the highway's progress was checked by more frequent towns but was no less stunning in its sweeping seascape. I thought about Julie, something I rarely let myself do. Julie and me. It had been, after all, seventeen years. *I should be able to think of her, see her, without being overwhelmed by pain.* And mostly, I found that I could. We'd been together—lovers, feminist-activist allies, roommates, friends—for five years. After graduation, we'd rented a duplex in south Minneapolis. I went to work at the *Minneapolis Star,* and Julie had a series of temporary jobs while she "decided about grad school." She had been considering social work or law. I wondered if she ever did go on.

In some ways, it had never been "okay." Julie was more conservative, more of a liberal to my radical. She was always preaching caution when I wanted to "storm the bastions." She wanted to talk people around while I wanted to shock people into perception. As the years went by, I grew more radical, and she grew more moderate. And as I became increasingly comfortable being a lesbian, coming out more and more, it seemed she grew less and less comfortable.

We still participated in or attended most feminist events and activities together those years immediately following our graduation, but we argued continuously. She talked about not alienating people while I flirted with separatism. I did civil disobedience while she refused to break the law.

"You're breaking the law," I insisted, "every time you speed. We all choose which laws we're going to abide by and which laws we're going to break. It's just a matter of priorities, Julie."

I threw closet doors open and turned on the lights while Julie retreated into the dark corners of her closets. And, as my drinking increased, the part I always wanted to forget the most, my mouth tended to get meaner and meaner. She would withdraw, and I would verbally punch at the vacuums created by her recession.

"Julie!" I might scream at her. "You can't just *not go* to pornographic movies. You've got to dramatically educate others about their content! About what they do to women and women's lives!"

"Can I just disagree with you, Tyler? I happen to think people have the right to choose whatever movie they want to see without being censored."

"Censored? Censored?" I'd roar. "Where did you get that bullshit?" About this time, I might move in close to Julie, my face inches from hers. "Is this that 'good liberal' crap you pick up at the Civil Liberties Union?" She was doing volunteer work there. "Oh, they're fabulous, aren't they? About people's rights, aren't they? As long as we're not limiting those good white liberal boys' rights to view women being abused, raped, humiliated, debased, beaten! What about *women's* rights? HUH? HUH? Where is your goddamned Civil Liberties Union then? And whose side are you on, Julie? Jesus christ, Woman!"

"Oh, leave me alone, Tyler," she'd respond, walking away from me. I knew I wasn't really helping matters; I knew I wasn't getting through to her when I screamed in her face. I just felt so helpless and desperate. I loved this woman, but I saw her slipping further and further away. And at the time, I didn't realize it probably had at least as much, if not more, to do with my drinking than with our different styles.

Our friends chose to spend less and less time with us.

A year or two after graduation, Julie got involved in a production collective that brought women's musical events to the Twin Cities. "Women's music" was radical back in the '70s, trying earnestly to combine art with politics—and often succeeding admirably. Women and their words—songwriting, performing, writing, publishing, bookselling, sharing philosophy, having poetry readings—all became the lifeline, the voice of the early Women's Liberation Movement.

And yet, I dismissed Julie's commitment to this part of the movement. "It's still about women," I complained to Mary Sharon, "without being *too* radical." I saw Julie's involvement as another withdrawal into an easy place. When I look back now, I think I had just worked myself into a state of mind where I found fault with everything she did.

She met Elaine there, who quickly became an installation around our house. Elaine had an ailing relationship, and somehow our home became her sanctuary. I didn't really mind. She was smart and funny, not hard to have around. She wasn't very interested in feminism, but she didn't resist it either.

Then one day, I came home from work and found a note from Julie. "Sorry," it read. Nothing else. No explanation. No softening of the blow. Her stuff was gone. Our record-and-tape collection decimated by her removal of those items she deemed to be hers. Books were toppled over on the shelves, others that once held them up having been removed. A few lonely hangers cringed where once her clothes had been hung, next to mine. All of the gradual accumulation of Elaine's things—her Jungian books, her supersized coffee cup, a handful of clothing, her collection of rocks—were also missing.

I remember walking around the house, dazed—staring at empty spots on walls where posters had been hanging, gazing at the meager kitchen collection that could actually be identified as "mine," repeating that one-word note over and over: sorry, sorry, sorry. I went on the first bender I'd ever been on—diving into endless and bottomless beer bottles, resurfacing only because Mary Sharon insisted. I did not know, then, that submerging myself in alcohol was going to become a common escape method for me. Not that I blame Julie for my drinking. Oh, no. I did that all on my own, although it took me some years to figure that out.

Julie. I'd never seen or heard from her since, all those seventeen years. Nor had any of us, until Rachel tracked her down to invite her to the reunion.

I'd made arrangements to pick Mary Sharon up at the Seattle airport. We headed north on Highway 5 through Seattle and beyond, to catch the ferry at Anacortes. Washington was a sharp, lush green punctuated by frequent explosions of flowers—tulips and irises, daffodils and calla lilies, as well as enormous shrubs of rhododendrons competing with rose bushes.

At first, the freeway gave us glimpses of Puget Sound, so filled with islands that it didn't come close to approximating the feel of an ocean. It reminded me of many of Minnesota's northern lakes, deep blue surrounded by hills of tightly crowded trees. The Olympic Mountains, reaching up through the mist hovering on the western side of the Sound, dispelled that illusion, however.

Mary Sharon and I ooh-ed and aah-ed our way northward in satisfying appreciation. Between our exclamations and frequent nuzzlings by Aggie, who was almost as glad to see Mary Sharon as I was, we picked up the comfortable threads of our easy connection.

"Actually, I do fish," Mary Sharon said, apropos of nothing, but I had no problem following her.

I shook my head. "I can't imagine that, Mary Sharon. How did this happen?"

"Oh, Celia did it first. She does these—what?—outdoorsy things. You know. I mean, you would think she'd been born in the country in middle America rather than that Valley-girl place she grew up in! She hikes. Now, she actually takes tourists on guided hikes . . ."

"Really?"

"Oh yeah. She knows all the names of wildflowers and bugs and trees. She loves that stuff. Euuww!"

"I guess you don't love it so much, huh?"

Mary Sharon smiled. "Well, I'm exaggerating a little. I don't mind getting out there once in a while. I just think I got enough of the great out-of-doors growing up. When you live in a small town, you are never more than a block or two from the country. I know the country. I appreciate it, even. I just don't feel too much desire to be rambling 'round in it all the time."

"But Celia does, huh?"

"Oh yeah. And, you know? It's kind of neat. I mean, I like to hear what all those things are, as long as I don't have to spend too much time with them. So she goes on her jaunts, and I stay at home and do what I do best."

"Which would be? No, let me guess. Read."

"You bet. Unless there's a big northeasterner blowing in off the lake or it's winter, you can find me most days in a rocking chair on the porch, my superbly 'shoe-d' feet . . ." I'd noticed that her signature shoes, L.A. Gear, were still with her, ". . . resting on the railing 'neath the screens, a book in my lap."

"And sometimes, you're not even reading, are you? Just snagged by the majesty of Lake Superior and not able to take your eyes off it, right?"

"That's so."

"But fishing?"

"Oh yeah. Well, like I said, Celia's into this outdoorsy stuff. We feed the fire all winter with wood she's chopped on our own land. Well, *your* own land." We smiled at each other. They'd been there for three years, leasing the place from me, but doing such a fine job of maintaining and improving it, it's hard to say whose land it was. "So, of course, she had to try fishing. And she loves it. Serves fish to the guests now, fish she's caught herself. Well, it was only a matter of time before she got me to agree to tagging along. Just once, you understand."

I laughed, glancing sideways at Mary Sharon. Her high-tops were bright yellow, echoing the equally bright yellow t-shirt she was wearing ("Hillary for President, '96" emblazoned across her chest) that was tucked into her very ordinary jeans and further subdued with a navy blue blazer. Her blond hair was actually blond, maybe the first time I'd seen it in its natural color, cut short and neat, all one length. Nothing about her much resembled the Mary Sharon I'd known these past twenty-four years.

"That place has changed you, hasn't it?"

She grinned. "You like this new preppy look?"

"Actually, it looks remarkably appropriate on you. Isn't that odd?"

"I don't know if it's the place, Tyler, or the job. It really is a little difficult to get people in a county with a population of about 3,500 to take you seriously as a lawyer if you look like a "Laugh-in" escapee. Or maybe it's Celia or even age. Whatever."

"Celia? Did she want you to dress differently?"

"No, no. I don't mean that at all. It's just that—mmm, how to say this? Being as settled as I feel I am in this relationship, as secure, maybe I just don't need to be so flamboyant anymore. Attention-grabbing. Rebellious. I did have a good run at it, you know."

"Oh yeah, I suppose twenty-some years is probably sufficient."

"So, my guess is—it's all of those things together." She listed them again, on her fingers. "Age, the love of a good woman, the desire to do a job, and the North Shore itself."

"And fishing?"

"Well," she threw her hands up in mock resignation. "Celia convinced me to come along, promised me I wouldn't have to bait any hooks or anything. And, you know, there's something incredible about being out on a lake in the stillness of early morning, watching the crimson sun rise dramatically over the trees, hearing the occasional plop of a fish that you're hoping is willing to sacrifice itself to your food needs, watching a mother loon with baby on its back glide by serenely, seeing an eagle or a hawk loop above the trees, watching a moose puff by, ignoring you. I like it."

"You make it sound pretty wonderful."

"Don't get me wrong. It's not as if I do this all the time. Maybe once every week or so. But I do like it. I even surprise myself."

We both laughed. "So you got a copy of the obit, too, mmm?" We hadn't really talked on the phone, saving our catch-up for this ride.

"Yup. I assume you're thinking the same thing I'm thinking, right?"

"That Grace's dad was, at least, a child molester?"

"Yup. Not too surprising though, is it?"

"No. I've been thinking about those years. Makes a lot of sense now, doesn't it?"

"Uh-huh."

"What kind of surprises me is that we never figured it out then, you know?"

"Well, we did, kind of. Don't you remember?"

I frowned, thinking. "I don't think so."

"Remember when Women's Studies was up and running finally, and we had to take the Intro course because we were all majoring or at least minoring? When we got to what we later called the 'incest week,' Grace never showed up at class all week. Actually, never showed up at the flat even."

"I do kind of remember this. Didn't we have a house meeting or something? Talk about confronting her, offering her our support?"

"Yeah, but Rachel talked us out of it. Rachel told us there was some really awful stuff about Grace and her family, but we had to respect her right to privacy. Let her tell us herself, if she chose to. Which she never did."

"Okay, it's coming back. Rachel was always so protective of Grace, wasn't she?"

"Yup. Looks like there was probably good reason to be. Do you remember how they got to be friends in the first place? I've been thinking and thinking and can't remember."

"Sure. They were both in the same dance school. I think about seventh grade."

"You'd think that Grace's parents, what little impression I have of them, wouldn't exactly approve of Grace being friends with someone like Rachel. Jewish was 'bad enough,' but radical firebrands, too?"

"You forget. Rachel is not only a Fineberg; she's a Wedlin on her mother's side. Old money. Minnesota legends. Like the Pillsburys. Or the Daytons. Just the kind of people that new-money types like Grace's parents would be impressed with, would want their darling daughter to hobnob with."

"You're probably right. But how do you know that Grace's parents were 'new money'?"

I shrugged. "Come on. The fact that they lived in Edina, new-money haven. The obit description. Her daddy didn't go East to a school an old-money boy would go to; he went to the University. Wanna bet?"

Mary Sharon squirmed in her seat, reaching back to scratch Aggie's ears. "No, you're probably right. Do you think Rachel sent an obit to everyone?"

"I don't know. Think we should bring it up?"

"To Rachel maybe. Not Grace. Unless it gets brought up. Is Grace coming? You talked to Rachel, didn't you?"

"Yeah, I had to get permission for Aggie to come." I was silent for a moment, focusing on the road. "Everyone's coming."

"Oh-ho! The long-lost Julie surfaces?" I nodded. "How did Rachel find her?"

"Apparently she lives right in Minneapolis. A suburb, actually."

"A suburb? Julie lives in a suburb?"

"Now, Mary Sharon, don't be a snob. You're the one who was always accusing *me* of that!"

"Yeah, and you were usually right. Dreadful snob it's true, but right. Come on, you telling me you didn't *savor* the fact that she lives in a suburb?"

"Okay, okay, I admit. I saved this tidbit until we were together because I knew you'd be as awful as I am about it."

"Which suburb?"

My grin widened. "Wayzata."

"Wayzata?" she shrieked. "Sheesh, Tyler, that *is* old money. What is she, married?" I was smiling broadly now. "Oh, my god! She is, isn't she?"

"Yup," I concurred. "She is indeed. Rachel tracked down her parents, remembered the little town where she'd gone to high school . . ."

"How could she remember that? Do you remember that?"

"No, but I lost a lot of details during my drinking years, you know. Anyway, remember? Rachel has an *incredible* memory. She found the parents, and they gave her Julie's address in the Cities. She's coming."

"A wasbian!" Mary Sharon said, almost reverentially, making me laugh. "How do you feel about all this, Ty? Her coming and her defection from our 'nation'?"

"I feel pretty odd, Mary Sharon. A little stupid, even. I mean, what? I've been carrying an idiotic torch all these years for a woman who isn't even a lesbian? I don't know. I guess I'm glad she's coming. Probably settle some of these feelings finally."

Mary Sharon nodded solemnly. "Yeah, you're probably right. What else do you know about her?"

"Nothing. She never called Rachel, just sent a note saying she'd be there."

"She never called her? They live in the same city, and she never called her?"

"Well, Mary Sharon, maybe they've lived in the same city for years. And she's never called her before."

"Yeah, but don't you think that's odd?"

"Less so, now that I know she's married. I guess she probably wanted to just erase her past."

"How did Rachel find out she's married, if she never talked to her?"

"Julie's mother told her."

"Why do you suppose she's coming, if she wanted to erase her past?"

"I don't know. Maybe she wants to reconnect with us. Even if only briefly. We were all pretty tight, after all. And maybe . . . ," I hesitated, wondering how much of this was just a kind of wishful thinking on my part, ". . . maybe she has some unresolved feelings, too."

"Mmmm," Mary Sharon said, and I could feel her eyes on me, but I didn't take mine off the highway. "And what about this Jill you're dating? You haven't told me much about her."

"*She's* not coming!"

"Well, I know that, Tyler. I just mean, how's it going between you two?"

I took a deep breath. "She's not the 'one,' Mary Sharon."

"No?"

"No. We're having a good time. There are some things I really love about this woman, but I know it's not going to work."

"What do you 'really love' about her?"

I half-laughed, half-snorted. "Sex." Mary Sharon laughed, too. "You get used to not having it when you're not having it, and you kind of forget just how stunning it can be. Or are you guys already in the bed-dead stage of your relationship?"

"We're doing all right in that department, thank you very much for inquiring," Mary Sharon replied, somewhat archly.

I smiled. "Good. Anyway, it's fine. More than fine, even."

"And?"

"I also love it that she's a recovering alcoholic. We have the same language, you know? The same understanding of lots of things. In some ways, we're more compatible than almost anyone I've ever gone out with. She loves books, jazz, Aggie, the ocean."

"And so? What's the problem?"

I let a beat of silence go by. "She's not so keen on feminism."

"Oh." After a moment, Mary Sharon said, "Is that absolutely necessary? I mean, couldn't you just concentrate on what you do share and not expect her to be everything you want?"

"Sure. That's what we're doing now. And it's okay, really. But it won't last, not long term, Mary Sharon. This is FEMINISM, not toothpaste squeezing. Feminism is my life. You know that. It's already causing us some tension, and we've only been seeing each other for three months. It's not going to work."

"You don't think she can be educated?"

I frowned and shook my head. "She's forty-eight, Mary Sharon. If she hasn't educated herself by now, it's probably not going to happen. And anyway, I don't think it would be good for the relationship: me, educator; her, student."

"Bummer."

"Yeah, it is. I think now that I'm gone, she's going to start evaluating this relationship and decide to get out while the getting out is relatively easy."

"Oh." After another pause, she jumped back to the previous conversation, "So this weekend should be fun, don't you think?"

"Yeah. I just spent the whole drive up here replaying those years, how we all met, the creation of the department, our activism, everything. You shared a room with Grace for two years, Mary Sharon, didn't she ever confide in you?"

"No. Except—remember how she was about being asexual? That was a huge clue, too, I think." I nodded my agreement. "And sometimes I'd come home, and she'd be in our room talking to Rachel, and they'd stop the minute I walked in."

"Yeah, they were pretty secretive. But god, she was funny, wasn't she?"

"Uh-huh. And clever. Remember the time that basketball player got away with rape, inconclusive evidence, the jury said?"

"Yes. As I remember, this was the first time you declared that you were going to go to law school and 'get those bastards.'"

She smiled and continued, ". . . and Grace got that idea that we should harass him? Every night we'd put signs on his fraternity's front lawn. 'A Rapist Lives Here.' 'Gary Allen Got Away with Rape and This Fraternity Doesn't Care.'"

"And —'Cowards and Bullies Rape, Is That What Frat Boys Are?' It was terrific, wasn't it?"

"Yeah. Good old Grace, she'd never speak up in class or join us in any public actions, but she did love that sneaking-around stuff."

"Do you think we ever changed anything?" I asked suddenly.

"Tyler. We've been over and over this. Who knows? It's true, we're still fighting the same fights. Women are still getting raped and beaten, victimized by glass ceilings (and as far as that goes, glass walls and floors), harassed at work, belittled at home, ignored, demeaned. What can I say? Is it better? Women, and even girls, are speaking up and out in ways they never did in past decades. I don't know. Like you say in your column, we 'keep putting one foot in front of the other.' What else can we do?"

I sighed. "Yeah, I guess. I just think of all that hope we had twenty years ago, how much faith we had that things were really going to change . . ."

"Tyler!" Mary Sharon shouted at me. "Are you trying to depress me before we even get there?"

"Okay, okay, I'll quit."

By that time, we had reached Anacortes. I maneuvered the car onto the ferry, and we were moving across the water. We leaned on the railing of the deck (poor Aggie had to stay in the car) and ooh-ed and aah-ed some more. All around us were thickly forested, emerald-colored islands, some of them rising like the tops of mountains—which they probably were, I guess—out of the inky water. It still seemed like a lake, because of the closeness of the islands, but the distinct odor of saltiness reminded me that we were on an enormous inlet of the biggest ocean in the world. The sky was dark and low, the water choppy and menacing. I was glad we were on such a large conveyance and wondered, briefly, about the size of Rachel's boat.

By two o'clock, the four of us—myself and Mary Sharon, Teddie and Julie—were waiting on the Lopez Island dock for Rachel to show up. It's very odd, seeing someone you haven't seen for nearly twenty years. It's a little like looking in a mirror with clear eyes, I guess, and suddenly seeing that you're not that sweet young thing in her twenties anymore (not that I was ever "sweet" exactly). We were twenty-five years old when Julie slunk away with her new girlfriend; now we were just a little short of forty-five.

Julie and I hugged each other; it seemed like the polite thing to do. After all, we had meant a lot to each other once. And then I checked her out, surreptitiously, while she hugged Mary Sharon and Teddie. She looked like Julie, and she didn't. Her brown hair displayed no gray but was paler looking, maybe just fading into gray, I thought. She was more attractive, I decided, with her face and body filled out and matured. Sure, there were lines around her mouth and eyes that hadn't been there twenty years ago, but they were appropriate and looked fine on her. And small oval spectacles were perched on her nose. It was, I decided, just a shock to see someone age from midtwenties to midforties with no gradual passage. I couldn't even remember the ways in which Mary Sharon had aged, I was so accustomed to how she looked.

What surprised me more than the aging process was Julie's style. In a way, she reminded me a bit of that girl who first came to a Women's Studies class looking like some kind of leftover from the fifties. Now, her hair was long and fluffed out around her face in a manner that Mary Sharon and I usually referred to as "big hair." She was wearing makeup again, and her clothes looked like they'd been plucked off a daytime talk-show hostess (or so I thought, unkindly)—a kind of salmon-colored pantsuit thing that hovered between glamorous and tacky.

Teddie, on the other hand, was still gloriously Teddie. Her nappy hair was cropped close to her head and shot through with grey. She was wearing her usual no-nonsense clothes: a pair of khaki pants with a black t-shirt. Her roundish body was rounder but didn't seem the least diminished in energy.

"Who's this?" she asked, leaning over Aggie. She looked slyly up at Mary Sharon and me. "I know I haven't seen Grace in a long time, but . . ."

"Teddie!" Mary Sharon shouted, laughing.

"I'm gonna tell Grace you said that!" I added, making the introductions among Aggie and Teddie and Julie.

"Look!" Teddie exclaimed, bouncing onto the next subject in true-Teddie fashion. She stuck her feet out toward us, resembling a toddler with new shoes. "I told this guy at the shoe store I needed some sturdy walking shoes for a trip out west, and he said these were the thing. What do you think?" I placed my own foot with my identical Tevas next to hers. "Ohmigod! You have the same shoe, Tyler! Is this the 'in' thing these days?" She looked at Mary Sharon and Julie.

"I don't have any," Julie responded, "but it does seem like they're pretty 'in.'"

Mary Sharon looked almost sheepish. "Yeah, I've got a pair, too."

"What?" I yelled. "You actually wear something besides L.A. Gear?"

"Occasionally. You gotta have shoes to stomp in and out of water up there in northern Minnesota."

Teddie was looking Mary Sharon up and down more carefully. "Hey, Mary Sharon! You've really changed, haven't you? What happened?"

Mary Sharon laughed. "Tyler and I just had this conversation. Spare me, okay? I'm just getting older."

"So, Mar Shar, just out of curiosity, what do you wear on your feet when you're practicing law?" I asked.

Mary Sharon grinned. "You just won't leave me alone, will you? Actually, I still wear my L.A. Gears. As long as I've toned down the rest, it seems like people in my area have allowed that I'm 'just a wee bit eccentric with those odd shoes.'"

Julie piped up, "You're an attorney?" When Mary Sharon nodded, Julie said, "So am I."

"Really? We have a lot of catching up to do, don't we?"

"And Tyler?" Julie turned to me, "You still look remarkably the same." I shrugged self-consciously, not knowing whether that was a compliment or not. I was wearing my usual comfortable clothes—purple sweatpants and a lavender shirt. "Except you're a lot more grey. And your hair's so short." The awkwardness between us was palpable. She hastened to add, "It looks good on you though," followed by a nervous laugh.

"Thanks," I ran my hand through my hair. "I like it, too. I like grey a lot. Have any of you seen Rachel lately? Well, I know you have, Mary Sharon." I explained to Julie and Teddie, "Rachel came to Mary Sharon and Celia's B&B last summer when I was there." I might as well have said out loud to Julie, *some of us have stayed in touch.* "Oh, her dark hair, big surprise, is divinely peppered! And yours," I said, running a hand over Teddie's stubble, "is greying very nicely, too."

Mary Sharon sighed dramatically. "Not mine. Us Scandinavians? Our hair just recedes from blond to drab nothingness."

"Yeah, mine, too," Julie agreed. "It was getting so blah before I started coloring it." None of us had anything to say to that. I carefully did not look at Mary Sharon, as I knew Julie would interpret such a look between us as judgmental. Of course, she would've been right. Wasting time and money on dyeing hair was unthinkable to the two of us.

Mary Sharon turned to Teddie and teased, "No locks? Braids?"

"Naw," Teddie shook her head. "I leave that to my girls. I'm one damn busy woman, Mary Sharon. I got to have me the wash-and-wear Cadillac of hairdos. This does me just fine." She ran her own hand across her head.

"How are your girls, Teddie?" I asked, aware that I was still tweaking Julie.

Teddie shook her head. "Girlfriend, we are approaching adolescence. You don't even *want* to know the answer to that question!"

"You have kids?" Julie asked.

Teddie nodded, but before we got a chance to talk further, a large boat drew up alongside the dock, and a woman shouted, "Hey, someone catch this rope?" Teddie, of course, was the first to move and grabbed the rope that was tossed to her. "Are you Rachel

Fineberg's friends?" We nodded, and she said, "Jump aboard then. I'm your taxi."

We hesitated. I felt a little silly, but we didn't know this woman. "Rachel said she was picking us up herself."

"Mary Pensak, at your service," the woman on the boat introduced herself. "It's getting wild," she waved toward the water, "and Rachel was a little worried about taking her boat out in this weather—it's a lot smaller than mine. So she called me and asked me to do the honors. She said you'd know it was okay when I told you that Mary Sharon Shlut should go first. Does that make sense?"

We all laughed and tossed our bags to her, scrambling on board, Mary Sharon helping me to heave a reluctant Aggie up with us. We were off in minutes with our taxi driver telling us we didn't want to waste any time because a big storm was coming. I felt the thrill of adventure as I faced forward into the stiff gale at the front of the boat. Even in the greyness of a low sky, the wooded and rocky islands rearing up out of the increasingly frenzied sea were indescribably beautiful.

It only took about fifteen minutes to get to Rachel's island, luckily. Julie was not looking very well, and Aggie definitely did not like this motion. The boat lurched over each peak of water, then slapped down into the trough between these mountains. The ferry had been so large, there had been no sense of this much rolling and rocketing. I had no idea how little Rachel's boat was, but I assumed her judgment was good and was glad we weren't in it.

Rachel's pier was in a small bay that afforded some shelter. The boat tied to it was minuscule in comparison to the one we were on; I shuddered to think of us on the open sea in it. Our captain tried to hold the boat as steady as she could while we hauled our bags and selves out onto the dock, which was much smaller and lower than the one at the public landing on Lopez. She handed a shivering Aggie down to me. The wind was roaring now, whipping the sea into increasing turbulence.

"Will you be okay, Mary?" Teddie asked. "Maybe you should stay here until it dies down."

Our chauffeur shook her head. "I'll be fine, thanks. I'm not far from here. But I gotta go now. Just follow that path up the hill, and you'll find the cabin."

We shouted thanks and waved good-bye while starting up the hill. The wind made conversation difficult, as did the steep incline, so we didn't talk. At the top, we found ourselves facing the back of the cabin—a log structure that evoked images of romantic hideaways, even in this increasing maelstrom. We hurried across to the door just as a spattering of heavy raindrops began to fall.

And suddenly, there was Rachel in the doorway, spreading her arms to welcome us, backing up so we could crowd inside. Everyone was talking at once and hugging one another.

"I'm so glad you got here before the rain started!"

"The Strait is whipped to a fury."

"This was a terrific idea, Rachel."

"I need a bathroom," uttered a pale Julie, and Rachel rushed her off.

"Seasick," Mary Sharon stated the obvious.

"Uh-huh," I agreed. "It was rough out there."

"Grace!" Teddie shouted, making us all jump. "Where are you?"

"I'm right here," Grace said, standing in a doorway behind us. There was a surprised silence for a second or two when we turned, then we were all rushing to her, hugging and laughing and talking again.

"My god!" Grace said, staring at Mary Sharon. "Who are you, and what did you do with Mary Sharon Andrews?"

"Hah!" Mary Sharon responded. "You should talk! Are you related to the late Grace Stone, that renowned hippie?"

It was true, Grace didn't much resemble her college self. For one thing, an extremely beautiful woman had been hiding under that uncombed, unwashed hair. I don't think I'd ever thought of Grace as pretty, but here she was, standing in front of me like someone you'd expect to see in the movies, except for the lack of makeup. Belying Mary Sharon's statement about blonds going drab, her hair was a stunning snow white. She wore it pulled straight back from her face in a casual but tidy bun. Her eyes were clear and steady, but there were dark smudges under each one. I wondered if her father's death was difficult for her. She was wearing what appeared to be, at least to me, very expensive, although deceptively simple, clothes—white leggings with a white knit shirt and a cotton navy sweater looped over her shoulders in a manner that I always thought only rich women could successfully pull off. How could that be? Did wealthy daughters go to sweater-draping classes, or were they just born with the correctly sloped shoulders for perfect draping?

"And you two," Grace reached out to Teddie and me, "look just the same."

"Oh, great," Teddie said, "I'm still the perky cheerleader . . ." she poked her index fingers in her cheeks and smiled broadly.

"And I'm still the lumbering giant," I finished, walking around the room stooped over with arms hanging loosely, grazing the floor. These were familiar postures that we had adopted in our college days.

Grace laughed and said, "You two! It's so comforting to have some things not change."

Rachel had returned, as gorgeous as ever, I thought. She'd let her hair grow a little, and it was a riot of curls, sprinkled—as I'd said earlier—with flecks of silver. Tucked in her ringlets, on the top of her head, were a pair of multicolored half-glasses. Her smile, with the even, white teeth of expensive orthodontia, was still generous, and her gestures were warm and gracious. She seemed perfectly confident of her place in the world. She looked, as always, both casual and elegant, in soft gray corduroys and matching turtleneck. "Oh, it's so good to have you all here. For heaven's sakes, Tyler, straighten up. You look like a gorilla." I exaggerated my posture more, and Teddie went into a cheerleading position, chanting her favorite cheer:

"Roses are red,
Violets are blue,
Your farts stink,
And so do you!"

Mary Sharon put her arm around Rachel's waist and started walking into another room, saying, "I think you might have left those two in the zoo, Rachel. It's unkind, you know, to make them try to pass as human."

I started to make pseudomonkey noises, and Teddie upped her chanting, "Your farts stink, your farts stink!" as we followed Rachel and Mary Sharon into the living room.

Grace brought up the rear, saying, "Don't encourage them! They'll be like this all weekend," at which point I threw my arms around her and made snuffling noises in her neck while Teddie linked arms with her and jumped up and down, saying, "Go team, go! Kill the foe!"

"Oh, god!" Grace exclaimed. "I take it back. Really! You're nothing like you were twenty years ago. You've changed immensely. I wouldn't have recognized you."

Teddie immediately stood calm and cool, tucking her t-shirt back in her pants. "I know. I never thought that cheerleader label fit me at all."

I stood erect and said, "Why, it hardly seems possible that it's been twenty years, does it?" At which point, the five of us dissolved into laughter.

When our mirth subsided, Mary Sharon raised her eyebrows and asked, "Julie?"

"She's throwing up," Rachel informed us.

"Good," I said, my eyes growing wide the minute that single word slipped out. I clapped both hands over my mouth and mumbled, "Joke. Bad joke."

"Uh-huh," Teddie said languidly. "Are we, by any chance, harboring some long-buried hostility that's just finding its way to the surface?" I shook my head, feeling horrified that I'd let such an unkind thought find voice.

"She'll be all right in a few minutes," Rachel said.

"Julie or Tyler?" Mary Sharon asked, and I glared at her while the others chuckled.

Teddie changed the subject. "Rachel, this place is stupendous. Especially this incredible view."

She was right. The living room reached across the front width of the cabin, with a row of windows looking across a jumble of massive rocks that cascaded some hundred or so yards down to the now wildly churning waters of the Strait of Juan de Fuca. Even with the tremendous wind driving rain against the windows horizontally and visibility nil because of the thick fog and low clouds and darkening afternoon, it was clear that this cabin was on a spectacular vantage point.

The room itself was low-ceilinged with knotty pine walls and divided into two sides, bifurcated by the single door into the kitchen. On one end was a huge, solid, wood table flanked by windows on two sides and bookcases, which covered all the walls under the windows. Balancing this table on the other end was an enormous stone fireplace with a fire blazing in it. There were comfy-looking couches facing each other by the fireplace and two wicker chairs pulled close to this grouping. In the center, a large, low table held vegetables and dip, cheese and crackers, teeny sandwiches, and other delicacies scattered across it.

"Food!" Teddie exclaimed, settling onto one of the couches and beginning to munch.

Julie came back into the room, took one look at the food, blanched, and left again. We all looked at one another, and Mary Sharon said, "I'll check her."

I curled up on the couch across from Teddie while Aggie gratefully collapsed in front of the fireplace, checking me first to make certain I looked like I was going to stay. Rachel slipped her loafers off and settled on the other end of my couch.

"Mmmm," Teddie mumbled with her mouth full, "this is great. Thanks!"

Grace pulled her navy sweater over her head, sat down on one of the wicker chairs, and rearranged her bun. "Aren't you going to eat?" I asked, as I was putting together a plate for myself.

She smiled. "We've been eating since we got here."

"When did you arrive?" Mary Sharon asked, slipping onto the couch next to Teddie.

"Two days ago," Grace answered. "If I'd known I had just been recruited as slave labor, I would've come up with you all."

"Oh yeah, listen to her," Rachel said. "She lay on this very couch for two days while I cleaned the place and cooked my head off."

Grace, without the slightest sign of being ruffled, said, "I made the veggie dip."

"That's true. You certainly did," Rachel agreed.

Julie rejoined us, sitting in the other wicker chair. "I'm sorry," she said. "I'm not very good in a boat." We all made reassuring noises, and she asked, "Could I just have some plain crackers?"

"Oh, sure," Rachel jumped up. "I'll get them with the drinks. What does everybody want? I've got beer, wine, pop, juice, water. Coffee or tea, if you want. Whatever."

"Water will be fine for me," Julie said.

"Give me a beer," Teddie announced.

"I know, coffee for you, Grace," Rachel supplied. "Mary Sharon? Tyler?"

Mary Sharon said, "Coffee sounds great."

And I said, "Seven-up or Coke would be nice. Whatever pop you have."

"Rachel's got your favorite beer, Tyler," Grace informed me, as Rachel moved toward the kitchen.

I sighed. Might as well get it over with. "Thanks. I don't drink beer anymore." After the slightest of pauses, I continued, "I don't drink any liquor anymore. I'm a recovering alcoholic."

Everyone was silent as I fidgeted with a green pepper. "Well," Grace said brightly, "this should be informative, shouldn't it?" And we all laughed a little, breaking the tension.

"**L**et's take turns updating each other," Teddie enthused, when Rachel came back with the drinks.

"Oh, goody," Grace mocked, "just like a Women's Studies class. We can 'share.'"

"Grace," Rachel said, lightly slapping Grace's hand. "Don't be a spoilsport. I think it's a great idea. Why don't you go first, Thea?" Rachel had always refused to use Teddie's nickname, creating her own instead. Teddie shot her a look of affection.

"Okay," she agreed, waving her hand to indicate she had to finish chewing her last bite. "Should I start at graduation or where I am now?"

"Whatever you want," Mary Sharon encouraged.

"Some of you will know this . . . Okay. I'm the executive director of an organization called The Sojourner Truth Foundation. We fund, on a national level, women's organizations that are either serving women of color or are working on the conflation of sexism and racism. And all the other isms, too, of course. We also fund and/or initiate research and educational projects that have to do with women and racism. We're based in D.C. Most of you know I went out to Washington shortly after graduation to work on Barbara Jordan's staff . . ."

"Yes," Rachel interrupted, "some of us remember that more keenly than others."

"Jeez, Rachel, are you still angry about that?" Teddie teased. Rachel just smiled. "Anyway. I have two daughters. Sula is eleven, and Celie is ten. Yes, they're named after characters in Toni Morrison's and Alice Walker's books," she interrupted herself before any of us could ask. "I adopted them. They are beautiful, intelligent—too intelligent for me most of the time, have been the blessing of my life, and are giving me preadolescent jitters these days. They're with my parents in Boston right now, wrapping them completely around their little fingers, as they always do. That's about it, Girlfriends. My life is full and busy. Between work and the girls, not much time for anything else."

"No love life?" Mary Sharon asked.

Teddie shrugged. "Not much. After I went to Washington . . ." she looked a little sheepish before continuing, "I actually tried to go straight." We laughed. "Well, I figured I just loved Rachel, which didn't necessarily mean I was a lesbian." We laughed some more. "I was wrong, of course. Or the men I dated were. Anyway, I finally went back to women and stayed with Janice, the first one I fell in love with, for about eleven years—although it wasn't good for about ten of those years." We raised our eyebrows, smiled, shook our heads, and—at the same time—nodded our understanding.

"So, you were with this woman when you adopted the girls?" Julie asked.

"Sort of," Teddie agreed. "We didn't ever live together. She had to live in New York because she's an actor. She thought I should move there, and I insisted that I had to be in D.C. to do the work I was doing. That was pretty much of a stalemate. It got worse, of course, after the girls, because I couldn't take the train up for weekends anymore, and—when she was working—she obviously couldn't come down on weekends. Well, it was ridiculous really. In many ways, we were wild about each other, but we wanted different things . . . Finally, I just called it quits. It was too chaotic for me and, even more important, for the girls. And since then—" she shrugged elaborately, "I go out occasionally but haven't really gotten involved. My girls fulfill my intimacy needs, I guess. And I just don't have much extra time. Relationships take a *lot* of energy."

Mary Sharon was next. "Remember when we graduated, the women's shelters and rape crisis centers were just popping up all over? For almost fifteen years, I worked for one or another of those agencies, still in Minneapolis, in every possible capacity, from intake clerk to director. I loved it but kept feeling like I wanted to approach this issue of violence from a different perspective. When Clare and I broke up—remember Clare?" We all nodded. "We'd been together for ten years; I decided to go to law school. At the same time, I wanted a drastic change, so I applied in the San Francisco area, got accepted at Hastings, and moved in with Tyler."

"Living together, just like college." Julie grinned.

"Not exactly, but certainly similar. Tyler has this house with a studio apartment. So I had my own space, but—of course—we visited back and forth a lot. It was great. I worked at an agency that served women who were victims of violence, and eventually I fell in love again. Her name is Celia. Three years ago, after I finished law school, Celia and I came to Minnesota to visit my mother—my father died a year before that—" we murmured sympathetically, "and Tyler was there because her mother had just died." I felt a lump form in my throat and thought, *Jesus, it never quits.* There were more sympathetic sounds. "Well, to make a long story slightly shorter: Celia and I fell in love with the North Shore of Lake Superior. Tyler had just inherited a house there but was not ready to abandon San Francisco, so we leased her house and turned it into a B & B."

"Wow!" Teddie said. "Let's have our *next* reunion there!"

Rachel inserted, "It's a stupendous place. I was up there last summer, just for a weekend. But I can assure you, I'm going for a longer visit this year!"

"It's true, it's a very special place," Mary Sharon was looking at me with shining eyes, "and Celia and I are really happy there. I practice law in the little town of Grand Marais and do pro bono work for the local violence agency. Celia and I seem very settled with each other. We've been together four and a half years now. So. That's the short version." And she turned to her left where Julie was sitting.

Julie smiled a tight little smile. It was a familiar gesture to me: she was nervous. "Well," she hesitated, taking a sip of water and pushing her glasses tighter against the bridge of her nose. "It's been a lot of years." She smiled that nervous smile again. "I don't really know where to begin." She glanced at me and then away, and I thought—you could begin with your wicked two-timing of me— and then mentally laughed, chiding myself for sounding like a country western song.

"After Tyler and I broke up . . ." Julie did not look at me this time, and I thought she'd better not. I did not call it "breaking up"—as if it were a mutual decision—when one took off with a friend and simply left the other one a note saying "sorry." ". . . I lived in Iowa City while Elaine was getting her MFA in writing. After her degree, we moved to New York. Mostly what she wanted. I hated it, so eventually I came back to Minnesota."

She sipped her water again, not making eye contact with any of us. We all glanced at one another and waited. "Well. Anyway. I went to law school, too. I'm an attorney. My specialty is sexual harassment." We breathed noises of approval. "And I'm married."

This was received in total silence. Julie was still not looking at us and finally Rachel took pity on her and said softly, even though she obviously knew because she'd been the one to tell me, "I guess 'married' means to a man?"

"Oh. Yeah . . ." Julie nodded. She wasn't the first lesbian I'd known who'd been caught up in the fervor of those early feminist days and later went back to men, but still . . . Fleeting memories of the two of us in bed slid through my mind, and it seemed inconceivable that she had left that all behind. What amazed me the most was that she was so hesitant, so unsure of herself. What had happened to that sharp mind? That quick tongue? That determined woman who was never afraid to stand up to me when few would?

"Uh," Grace faltered a little, "how long . . ."

Julie smiled slightly, taking a breath. "It's been seven years now. We have two kids: a little girl named Jessica, she's five, and a three-year-old boy named . . ." she hesitated for a moment, shooting a quick look at me, ". . . Tyler."

I felt a stab of astonishment. "Does your husband know . . . ?"

"Oh sure, Tyler," she answered more easily now, seeming to relax somewhat. "What kind of a marriage would it be if he didn't? I wanted to name our girl Tyler, but . . . that was just a little too much for him." She smiled, almost a real smile.

"Well," Mary Sharon said kindly, "it has been many years, hasn't it?" And we all relaxed a little.

"So I guess working and having kids must take up most of your time, mmm?" Teddie asked, and I knew—and probably everyone else did, too—that she was fishing, trying to find out if Julie did anything else political, besides her job.

"Well, yeah," Julie agreed, "it does take most of my time. I do some volunteer work, though. For instance, I'm an AIDS buddy. It's important, you know, that my kids learn about community service."

"What's an AIDS buddy?" Mary Sharon asked.

"It's part of a hospice program for AIDS patients and resembles the Big Brother/Sister program. We more or less 'adopt' an AIDS patient, standing in as family/friend/caregiver to him or her."

Rachel said, "Yeah, I know about that program. It does terrific work." Julie smiled, looking relieved.

"I guess it's my turn," Grace said, moving us right along. "I think you all know I moved to Seattle right after graduation. I've only been back to Minnesota once, some years ago, not even for my father's recent funeral. The old bastard." She said this calmly, dispassionately, dissuading any of us from reacting sympathetically. "I've seen Rachel from time to time because she comes out here to the island, but I've not kept up with any of you. I hope you understand, that was never meant to be personal. I simply wanted to break from almost everything to do with Minnesota. I run my own business now. I have a lovely old Victorian on Queen Anne hill that has stupendous views of the Sound. I'm . . . not unhappy."

Not unhappy? What an odd way, a Grace-way to put it, I thought. "What kind of business?"

After a barely noticeable hesitation, she answered, "I run a temp agency."

"Still no love life?" Teddie asked, wiggling her eyebrows lasciviously.

Grace shook her head, smiling. "You guys never did listen to me. I told you more than twenty years ago: I choose asexuality. Period. Nothing's changed."

Teddie gaped at Grace. "You really have not had any love life all these years?"

"Really."

"It looks like I might be the old lady of love lives here," Rachel said, breaking our focus on Grace abruptly, something—I realized with a start—she'd always done. She pulled her glasses off her head and slowly wiped them with her turtleneck. "Back to the beginning first: when Thea broke my heart."

Teddie interrupted, rolling her eyes, "You know, Ms. Fineberg, you could've come with me to D.C. Your heart wasn't the only one broken." And they smiled fondly at each other.

"Anyway," Rachel continued, "I just dug into my work. I was in a research lab, working on viruses at that time. Prior to AIDS, of course, but we were looking at retro-viruses, which is what AIDS is. Fascinating stuff. There was this woman . . ." We all laughed. "Anyway, her name is Robin, and we've been together for nineteen years now."

"Wow!" Mary Sharon said. "I'm impressed. And inspired."

"And Girlfriends?" Teddie leaned toward the rest of us conspiratorially. "You get that number? Nineteen? I mean how *broken* was her heart, after all?" She leaned back and directed her next remark toward Rachel. "I mean, sounds to me like I did you a mighty big favor."

Rachel smiled broadly. "That may be so, Thea. Anyway, Robin had a little girl who was just two at the time, so we raised her together. Meg—named after Meg Christian—is twenty-one now. She just finished college with a degree in communications and is trying to figure out what's next."

"You never had custody problems?" Julie asked.

"No. Robin's ex was a peace and justice activist who gave lip service, at least, to feminism. It would have tarnished his reputation if he'd objected. We've always assumed it bothers him more than he admits, but Meg is a terrific kid, so there's not much he can truly complain about. Anyway, the more research I did, the more I got interested in medicine, so when I was thirty I went to med school. Now I'm a doctor."

"Tell them about the clinic," Grace prodded.

Rachel smiled at Grace. "I've got lots of money. You all know that. It's not as if I need to make more. So I started a free-clinic in a low-income neighborhood. I serve, almost exclusively, women and children. Family practice. It's the passion of my life."

"Oh, Rachel," Teddie breathed huskily. "That's wonderful! I always knew you'd do something wonderful."

"And that leaves you, Tyler. Last but certainly not least," Rachel said.

"Well. When Julie broke *my* heart . . ." I started, and we all laughed. *Only,* I thought to myself, *she really did break my heart. Only, if I'm completely honest with myself, I didn't do much to unbreak it.* "Actually, the longest relationship I ever had was with Lady Liquor. And believe me, it was a destructive love/hate kind of thing. I was already drinking, periodically, too heavily in college, some of you will remember," I glanced meaningfully at Julie, "and it just kept getting worse. I haven't had a drink in seven years now."

I jumped when they all clapped and cheered. Even though it was sappy, my eyes got all wet, and Mary Sharon reached across the table with a napkin. I dabbed at the moisture and said, "I love you guys, you know that?"—my eyes immediately getting wetter.

"Yeah, yeah," Grace said, "We know that. Enough of this drivel now," while Teddie wiped her eyes, too.

I took a deep breath, blowing my nose. "So, aside from that constant companion, the bottle, I haven't really had any lasting relationships. Julie," I nodded toward her, "was the longest." And then my eyes softened, and I found myself letting go of some of the pain I'd been so churlishly nursing all those years. "You really were the love of my life, Julie." And she smiled, a real smile, a sad smile. "So there've been other women, some even for two or three weeks . . ." Everyone laughed. "But, lest I sound pitiful here, I do have my work, and I do love it. I worked for the *Minneapolis Star,* as you mostly know, right after graduation. When Julie left, I went home to California. I got a job with the *San Francisco Chronicle* right away. I've been writing my syndicated column, "Womenswords," for twelve years now. And I've done a nonfiction book, sort of a collection of my columns with extended analysis and facts plus a series of first-person testimonials from women who've survived violence. *The Undeclared War: Violence Against Women* is the name of it. I just had my first novel published last year and am working on a second one. I've worked for various feminist agencies over the years. That's about it."

"Let me tell you," Mary Sharon interjected, "Tyler has worked tirelessly for so many women's issues and has won numerous awards and accolades, not to speak of a Pulitzer for a series she did for the *Chronicle* on cops and violence, and what was the one for *Undeclared War?*"

"Meet my agent, Folks," I said, and we all laughed. "The Susan B. Anthony Award for best nonfiction, thank you very much, Mary Sharon."

"Wow!"

"Congratulations!"

"What's the name of your novel, Tyler?" Julie asked.

"*Leaving Home.*"

"Well," Rachel said, "I must confess, it's not surprising at all to find that we're such an illustrious group." *Except Grace,* I thought. *She's not doing anything political, anything particularly exciting even. But then . . . I guess our expectations were always lower for her than for anyone else.* "How about some real food now?" We all groaned but helped clear away the hors d'oeuvres and set the table for the main course—a meatless chili, slabs of delicious bread—"No, no, I didn't make it," Rachel said, "I bought it at a fabulous bakery at Friday Harbor on San Juan Island."—and a salad.

The storm continued to buffet the cozy cabin, with the wind howling, the rain slashing against the windows, and brilliant flashes of lightning and deafening thunder occurring at regular intervals. Both Grace and Rachel marveled at the electric works, informing us that lightning storms were *most* uncommon in the Northwest, insisting that this was a freak event staged just for our presence. We sat around the table, laughing and talking, asking one another more details about our lives, and passing the food around, again and again.

Whenever the lightning flared, we could see the trees and rocks outlined outside. During one such blaze of light, Teddie—who was facing the windows on the opposite end of the cabin from the fireplace—suddenly jumped to her feet, knocking her chair over and yelling, "There's someone out there!"

"What?" We all turned toward the now-darkened window.

"There was someone out there," Teddie repeated, more calmly. She was still standing. "I saw a figure in the lightning, just a little ways out from the cabin." Lightning crackled again, and we all looked out the window: there was no one there.

"That's impossible, Thea," Rachel said calmly. "No one but us is on the island. And certainly no one could have landed on it in this storm. You must have seen a tree and mistaken it."

"I'm telling you," Teddie insisted. "I've been looking out that window every time the lightning flashes, and I know what the trees out there look like. This wasn't a tree. It was a person." She was insistent, and because Teddie wasn't taken to fancy, we all felt uncomfortable.

"What do you think we should do?" Grace asked.

Teddie righted her chair and said, "I don't know. Wouldn't he come to the door if he wanted shelter?" And I thought, and wondered if others were thinking the same thing, *what does he want if he doesn't want shelter?*

Rachel said, "Let me check the back door." The front door was in the room with us, and it was clear there was no one there. "Let me go with you," I volunteered.

"No, I will," Mary Sharon jumped up and darted into the kitchen.

In a moment, Mary Sharon and Rachel were back, Rachel shaking her head. "It's too dark to see anything outside," she strode over to the front door and locked it, an action that made me feel a little uneasy, "but no one was at the door." She shrugged.

Mary Sharon sat down, and I looked at her quizzically. "I just didn't want *you* to be the one to go look." I thought I knew where this was going, so I didn't respond.

Grace looked from Mary Sharon to me and said, "Come on, you two. What's up?"

I glared at Mary Sharon, who said, "They might as well know. You just shouldn't have invited Tyler, Rachel. She has a habit of stumbling across bodies. *Dead* bodies."

"I'd hardly call it a habit," I protested.

The rest of the dinner, of course, was given up to discussing the murders I'd gotten accidentally involved in—one in California, the other in Minnesota. I'd only been peripherally connected to either incident, but Mary Sharon was convinced that I was some kind of a jinx because, after all, most of us never have the experience of encountering one, let alone two, corpses. What I didn't know, however, was that I was about to "stumble across" yet another dead body.

"**R**achel, have you got a phone or anything?" I asked. "In case . . . " I shrugged, not wanting to actually voice my concerns out loud as well as not exactly knowing, anyway, what those concerns were.

Rachel shook her head but said, "Yes and no. There's no phone service to the island but . . ." she fished in a voluminous bag and pulled out a cell phone, "Voila! Modern technology!" She flipped it on and said, "Of course, there's nothing but static on the line now, but it will be okay when the storm blows over."

After dinner and cleanup, we explored Rachel's cabin and hauled our stuff around to our sleeping areas. Off the kitchen were a bathroom and bedroom, which Rachel and Grace were sharing.

Upstairs, tucked under the eaves, were two more bedrooms—one with a double bed and one with twin beds. Mary Sharon and I took the double bed, and Teddie and Julie took the twin beds.

I tried, in vain, to get Aggie to go outside. She stuck her nose out in the howling wind and sheets of rain just as an ear-splitting clap of thunder occurred, and she quickly retreated away from the door. After juggling our own needs for the one bathroom, we all headed for bed. When I got upstairs, I found Mary Sharon in the dark, peering out the low window. I turned on the light, making her jump.

"What are you doing?" I asked, almost peevishly.

She got up from the floor, shrugging, her flannel nightie rippling from her shoulders down to her toes. "Just looking. It's amazing how much you can see when the lightning flashes."

"See anyone?" I was almost afraid to ask. She shook her head, climbing under the ancient, heavy quilt on our bed. The bed appeared to be made of thick tree branches. I grasped a post and shook it, saying, "You think this is safe?"

Mary Sharon, already snuggled deep in the recesses of the comforter, murmured, "I'm sure it is, Tyler." When I turned the light off and slid in next to her, she said, "What do you think Teddie saw out there?"

"No, Aggie, there's not enough room for three of us up here," I told Aggie, who was attempting to join us. Even in the dark, I could feel her doleful eyes on me, then I heard her crawling under the bed. She didn't like thunder. "Poor Aggie," I murmured, then turned my attention back to Mary Sharon. "I don't know. It seems likeliest that she saw *someone*. I mean, Teddie? She isn't exactly flaky, you know."

"I know, but how could anyone be on the island in this storm?" As if to punctuate her question, our room was filled with a brilliant light followed almost immediately by an unnervingly loud crash of thunder. Mary Sharon sat up in bed. "God, it's close. I hope it doesn't hit the cabin."

"So do I."

"Tyler," Mary Sharon prodded me as she curled back under the quilt, "answer me. How could anyone be here in these conditions?"

"I don't know, Mary Sharon," I answered, definitely peevish this time. "How should I know? I've been here the exact same amount of time as you. I've seen the exact same things you've seen. I know just exactly as much as you do."

"Come on, Ty, you're the big detective. What do you think?"

"Mary Sharon," I turned over, away from her, "I think we should go to sleep." I knew she just wanted to talk about it, that she could figure anything out that I could figure out, but I didn't feel like talking about it. I didn't feel like being the "big detective."

After a moment's silence, during which time I doubted I'd actually heard the last of Mary Sharon, she said, her voice low, "What a bombshell from Julie, huh? Even if we did already know."

This had the desired effect, and I turned back over. "I know. Still. I'm not entirely surprised."

"No?"

"No. I mean, in most ways, she was always more conventional than the rest of us." We were whispering, cognizant of the fact that the object of our conversation was just on the other side of the wall. "Maybe she was never really a lesbian, just got caught up with our zeal."

"You think?"

Again, I remembered Julie's body and mine coming together and shook my head. "No. I don't really think that's true, not when I think of us together. I guess what I think is—it was too hard for her to be a lesbian, too hard to 'swim upstream.' She never did tell her parents, remember? Was convinced it 'would kill them.' Know what I mean?"

"Uh-huh. But amazing that she named her son after you. Mmmm?"

"I'll say. I wonder what her husband really thinks." After a moment I added, "Grace was sort of vague, wasn't she?"

"Yeah. Just like always. That woman doesn't want to get close to anyone."

We talked for a few more minutes about the rest of the group before drifting off to sleep. The thunder and lightning subsided while we were still talking, but the rain seemed to continue all night. I slept uneasily, always being lulled back to sleep by the loud patter on the roof.

It was still drizzling and grey when Aggie's nose prodded me insistently. Thinking of her refusal to go out the night before, I knew her need was monumental. I stumbled out of bed and pulled on a pair of sweatpants with the t-shirt I'd worn to bed, and—carrying shoes and socks—carefully made my way down the steep, narrow, curving stairway to the first floor.

Rachel was up, making coffee. We smiled and hugged one another. In low tones, Rachel said, "It is *so* good to see you, Tyler."

"Ditto," I replied. "We really shouldn't wait so long."

"You're right. Want some coffee?"

"I'd love some, but I have to get Aggie out first."

"You can't just let her out?"

"Yes, but she won't move away from the door. We have our routine."

As I pulled a sweatshirt on, Rachel said, "It's still raining a little. You'll find a slicker by the back door."

I mouthed "thanks" and stepped into the lean-to behind the kitchen. I pulled on a bright yellow slicker and went out the back door with Aggie, who immediately squatted and relieved herself. *Damn,* I thought to myself and said aloud, "I'll be right back,

Aggie," and darted back into the house to use the bathroom myself.

When I got back out, Aggie was waiting by the door for me, fully expecting me to return for our daily morning walk. This habit had begun her first year and still continued in this, her thirteenth year. Although she moved a bit more slowly now because of arthritis and general old age, she never wavered in her expectation that we do this each morning.

The wind was still fierce. I wasn't sure if it was actually raining or if the gusts were just blowing moisture off the trees. I walked around to the front of the cabin and gaped at the waves, which were smashing violently against the rocky shore, and at the immense beauty, even in this gloomy dawn, of a restlessly churning sea. In the distance, through the mist, I could make out a dark mound rising out of the water, presumably another island. It made me think of *Brigadoon,* wondering if it was still there on clear days.

There were paths going off into the woods on both sides of the cabin. Aggie and I struck off down one of them, the smattering of raindrops not deterring us. The trees were close—cedar, maple, and madrona—all dripping wet. I hoped it would get dryer sometime this weekend, as the island would be fun to explore. Rachel had told me the night before, it was about two miles long and little more than a half mile wide at any point. Aggie ventured off into the woods a little but never very far, mostly, I suspected, because it was unknown to her. She wanted to keep tabs on me, make certain I wasn't going to abandon her in this foreign place.

On one of her forays, she began to bark. *Oh no,* I thought, *this is all too familiar.* She only barked if there were people she didn't know or animals or a dead body, as in the one time she found one in the park across the street from our house in San Francisco. Now what? I wasn't sure which of those alternatives I preferred. "Aggie?" I called. Her barking continued.

I stopped, calling her name once more, and trying to think what to do. Go into the woods to see what she was barking at? Go back for reinforcements? Keep walking and hope that she'd just stop barking and come back to me? Just return to the cabin and pretend nothing had happened? I was acutely aware of the person Teddie had been sure she'd seen the night before.

I finally decided to continue walking and see what happened. After all, she was probably just reacting to a chipmunk or something. Aggie kept barking at first, then crashed through the woods to my side, where she whined and let out little yips when I tried to reassure her. It was clear she wanted me to follow her. "What do you think? That you're Lassie or something?" She kept whining. I took a deep breath and gave in, following Aggie into the drenched forest.

We didn't have far to go before we reached an escarpment sliding down some twenty or so feet into a rocky rift. On a ledge, about halfway down, directly below us, was a crumpled form. Aggie started barking again, as if to shout, "Get up!" and I thought, *Oh, no, Mary Sharon is never going to let me forget this.* Because I could tell that this man was never going to get up again. There was a hole in the middle of his back.

There was no blood that I could discern, but there wouldn't be—not with all the rain. It was possible to reach him; the cliff face was not too steep, but it was composed of loose rock, which made me loathe to attempt the descent. My bulky size did not easily lend itself to precarious footing in the best of conditions, let alone on rocks made slippery by rain.

"Okay, Aggie, okay," I placed my hand on her head. "You've made your point now. You can quit barking." She looked up at me questioningly and let out one final yap. "We'd better go get help."

I headed back to the cabin stealthily, aware of the possible presence of another person in these woods. A person with a gun. When I thought of the storm, I realized it wasn't just a possibility that someone else was here, it was almost a certainty. Unless the killer was one of us. And then I understood how absurd my "stealth" was, as if Aggie's noise hadn't heralded our presence already, loudly and clearly. I almost laughed at my theatrics, except I didn't feel willing to completely abandon my furtiveness. Such thoughts did relax me enough, however, to consider the situation. It really was too bizarre that I should find myself in this position again. Maybe Mary Sharon was right: there was something about me that attracted trouble. I mean, who finds three bodies in her lifetime?

I told Aggie to wait outside for me when we reached the cabin. A fire had been built, and Rachel and Grace and Mary Sharon were huddled in front of it with coffee. I stood in the kitchen door with the slicker still on, dripping on the floor.

Rachel jumped up. "Tyler! Take that slicker off and come over here and get warm." She brushed past me into the kitchen and was pouring me a cup of coffee before she looked closely at me. "What is it? Tyler? What's wrong?"

Mary Sharon and Grace joined us in the kitchen. I gulped some too-hot coffee, looking up at them from under my brows. I took a deep breath. "There's a man out there. I think he's dead."

"What!?" Rachel uttered.

Mary Sharon asked, seriously, "This isn't a joke, is it, Tyler?"

I rolled my eyes. "I wish."

"A man?" Grace, in silk pajamas, asked, then repeated, "A dead man?"

"The 'Body Finder' is in fine mettle, as usual."

"Mary Sharon!" I said sharply. "This isn't a joking matter. This guy is dead."

"Where is it . . . he?" Rachel asked.

"On a ledge, down the side of a gully or something. That way." I pointed in the direction from which Aggie and I had just come.

"I know the place. Are you sure he's dead? Did you check?"

"Well, I'm pretty sure. It looks like a bullet hole in his back." I was surrounded by the sharp intake of breath. "But I didn't check because the footing was too precarious. I didn't think two bodies were a good idea."

Rachel said, "Okay, I'll get some rope." She was pulling a jacket over her sweat suit. "You'd better wake the others. I think we should all go together."

Mary Sharon said, "I'll get Julie and Teddie," and started up the stairs while Grace disappeared into her bedroom, presumably to get dressed.

In about ten minutes, we were all assembled, a little sleepy and greatly confused. Rachel had gotten some rope and gloves, and we started off—Aggie and I leading the way. The sky was low and leaden, the wind was still sharp, but it didn't seem to be raining. I stopped to move branches off the path, obviously downed the night before. Alone, I had merely stepped over them, but now I took the time to toss them into the woods.

It didn't take us long to reach the spot where the undergrowth was drubbed, indicating where I'd entered the forest. At this point, Rachel said, "I think we ought to go single file here and try to disturb as little as possible. If Tyler is right about a bullet in the back, well, then it's murder. The investigators will not appreciate our messing up all the evidence."

"You're right, Rachel, but I do want to point out that the storm probably ruined most of the evidence already. And Aggie and I undoubtedly took care of the rest of it." She nodded, and we proceeded into the woods.

In a moment, we were looking over the edge of the precipice at the body on the shelf. It was only about ten or twelve feet from us, sprawled facedown.

Rachel was tying the rope around a tree and saying, "I'm going down to check him. Okay?"

"You're the doctor," Teddie said, and we all nodded in agreement.

It only took a moment for Rachel to reach his side. She steadied herself and pulled her gloves off, placing her fingers against his throat in search of a pulse. After a moment, she looked up at us and shook her head. She then knelt down next to the body and appeared to be scrutinizing it more closely. She slowly stood up, still staring at the body.

"Rachel?" I called to her, her stance seemed a little odd to me.

She said, without looking up, "I'm going to turn him over. I want to know if anyone recognizes this man."

When she turned him over, Grace emitted a low moan and stepped back. Teddie put her hand on Grace's arm and said, "You know him, Grace?"

Grace nodded, biting her lip slightly. Rachel quickly pulled herself up the rope and strode to Grace's side. "What is it, Grace?"

Grace looked at her, her dark eyes darker. "He's dead?"

"Yes. Definitely. Probably last night some time, although I can't be sure. The body would cool off quickly in a storm like this. Who is he, Grace?"

"A client of mine. But . . ." her hands reached up to rub her temples, as if she had a headache, "I haven't seen him for about a year."

"Okay," Rachel said, clearly to all of us. "I think we'd better go back to the cabin." She looked around for a minute. "Where's Julie?"

We all looked around. "I don't know," Mary Sharon said. "She was here a minute ago."

Rachel frowned and repeated, "Let's go back to the cabin."

"Are we going to just leave him there?" Grace asked in a small voice.

"I think the cops will want him to be as undisturbed as possible. In fact . . ." Rachel slipped over the edge again, letting herself down the rope, hand by hand. She turned him back over and arranged the body as much like it was as possible. Then she rejoined us, and we started back.

Just as we reached the door, Julie came puffing up the path from the bay where we'd docked the night before. Breathlessly she called, "The boat's gone! We're stuck here!"

Rachel went inside with Grace while the rest of us proceeded to the dock. Sure enough, the boat was gone. Mary Sharon and Teddie squatted down next to the rope that was still attached to one of the pilings.

"Cut?" I asked, expecting the worst.

"Hard to say," Teddie squinted at the rope, then held it up for Julie's and my perusal. "See how frayed it is? Could have just been the wind and water jouncing the boat around until the rope snapped."

Mary Sharon nodded and added, "That seems most likely. If anyone cut it, they had a very dull blade. Julie, what were you doing down here anyway?"

"Are you suggesting I set the boat loose?" she demanded to know.

"Actually," Mary Sharon said, "I wasn't even thinking of that. But, now that you bring it up, did you?"

"No! I came to make sure the boat was still here, to see if we could get off this island. I don't like the idea of hanging out with a dead body and a killer."

For a minute, none of us said anything, just stared at each other. I finally broke the silence. "We couldn't go anywhere anyway, Julie. We'll have to stay here until the cops come." Teddie nodded. I wondered if Julie had actually been thinking of getting in that boat and just leaving us all here, but then—when I remembered how sick she'd been last night—that seemed unlikely.

"But how are they going to get here?" Julie wailed.

"Get hold of yourself, Julie," Mary Sharon put her hand on Julie's shoulder. "Rachel has a cell phone, remember?"

"Yeah," Julie responded sullenly, moving away from Mary Sharon's hand, "if it works."

Her fears were soon realized, because when we'd trudged back up the hill to the cabin to find Grace huddled under a blanket in front of the fire, Rachel informed us, "The phone isn't working still. All I get is crackling."

"Let me see," Julie insisted. The phone made the rounds of all of our hands—each of us pushing buttons, shaking the instrument, tapping it against our fists—but nothing. We were stranded.

After a few moments of glum silence, Mary Sharon smacked her hands together and said, "Well. We still have to eat. If someone will point me toward the kitchen, I'll do the honors."

"I'll help you," I offered. I chopped onions and tomatoes and grated cheese for one of Mary Sharon's infamous omelets while she scrubbed and chopped potatoes and peppers. I did the sausage (Mary Sharon didn't "do" meat) and toasted thick slices of last night's bread in the oven while Mary Sharon made the omelets and potatoes.

"What do you think?" she asked in a low tone.

"I don't know." I glanced in the living room. Rachel and Grace were sitting near the fire, murmuring to one another. Teddie was staring out the window, and Julie wasn't in sight. Probably in the bathroom, I thought. "I feel like I'm in an Agatha Christie book."

"*Ten Little Indians.* Only that means one of us killed this guy and is going to continue killing all of us." I looked at her. "He must've been the guy Teddie saw last night, hmmm?"

"Maybe." I turned the bread over. "Or that might've been the killer."

"So you think the killer's still on the island?"

"That's an obvious possibility, isn't it? I mean, how could he get off in that storm?"

"Maybe he came in—if it is a 'he'—on a big boat and left the same way."

"Maybe. But remember? Our taxi driver was in a pretty big boat yesterday, and she was sure in a hurry to get into safe harbor somewhere."

"You don't think he took Rachel's boat?"

I shook my head. "Not in this sea. If he did, he's probably dead, too."

"But how did *both* of them get on the island in the first place? And why?"

"If there's two of them."

We silently tended to our food for a few minutes, then Mary Sharon asked, "You really think it could have been one of us?"

"Well, no, I don't *think* that. But—that doesn't mean it wasn't. I know it wasn't you, Mary Sharon, and that's the only thing I know for sure. Everyone else . . ." I shrugged. "We haven't seen most of these women for years. We don't know all that much about them."

"How do you *know* it wasn't me?"

"Because we slept in the same bed last night. I would've noticed if you got up and went downstairs. Someone did, though."

"Someone did what?"

"Went downstairs."

"You heard them?" When I nodded, Mary Sharon said, "Probably going to the bathroom."

"That's what I assumed."

"But *you* could've done it," Mary Sharon said, her eyes twinkling.

"Yep," I agreed. "This morning when I was out with Aggie. Maybe you should cross-examine Aggie."

"Yep," she agreed, and we smiled at each other just as Teddie came in.

"Can I set the table or something?"

"Good idea," I agreed, "We're just about ready here."

When we sat down to eat, Julie said, "Grace. I think you'd better tell us about this client of yours."

Grace narrowed her eyes, and Rachel said, "Uh-uh. Not now. After we eat."

Julie insisted, "I just think . . ."

"Not now," Rachel repeated so firmly that Julie desisted, but not without a sulky countenance.

There was some desultory conversation, but mostly we didn't even attempt to chat. Tension crackled between us, echoing the electrical tension of the storm the night before. While the others were clearing the table and washing the dishes, Mary Sharon and I slipped out the back door, on the pretext of walking Aggie.

"Whew!" Mary Sharon exclaimed. "A little strained in there, what?"

"No shit, Sherlock."

"Watson."

"What?"

"Watson. *You're* Sherlock, that makes me Watson, doesn't it?"

I rolled my eyes. "Whatever."

"Are we looking for something?" Mary Sharon asked, as we started down a path.

"I don't know. Maybe. Some sign of human presence other than ours, I guess."

"Otherwise one of us did it?"

I didn't answer her.

After a few moments, we broke free of the forest; the path we were traversing ended on the edge of a cliff above the roiling waters. Even though we were maybe forty or fifty feet above the water, the din from the crashing waves made conversation difficult.

"I wish it weren't so foggy and overcast," Mary Sharon yelled in my ear. "I bet the views are fabulous!"

"It's still gorgeous, though." I pointed to a low-flying eagle to our right. We watched in silence.

We walked along another path that swerved in and out of the trees, mostly keeping close to the edge of the land. Mary Sharon said, "We could get shoved over these cliffs, you know."

I stopped abruptly, Mary Sharon plowing into me from behind. "Now that's a loathsome thought, Mary Sharon. Do you think we ought to go back?"

"Naw. I just don't think we should go too close to the edge."

"As if you would anyway." Mary Sharon was terrified of heights. I wasn't terribly wild about them myself, but not as afraid of them as she was. "What are you thinking?"

"I was thinking that if we actually found something that someone didn't want us to find, THEN someone might want to push us over these cliffs."

"Mmm," I grunted agreement, picking my way over a fallen tree. *We read too many mysteries,* I thought to myself. "Mary Sharon?"

"Yeah?"

"Why do you think this keeps happening to me?"

"Who knows? It is kind of odd, isn't it?"

"That's an understatement. It's starting to give me the willies."

She nodded wordless understanding, then said, "Oh, oh. Look."

I followed the direction in which her outstretched finger was pointing and saw a small boat beached in the rocky cove below us. The path dipped downward, so we scrambled nearer to get a closer look. The boat seemed to be about the same size as Rachel's; it probably was hers. It was smashed against the rocks, two or three gaping holes in the bottom. The sea was pushing and pulling at the small craft, as if it were an encumbrance to be removed. We stood and watched this insistent action for a moment, and I kept thinking of a tongue working to dislodge a sliver of food from between teeth.

"You reckon this is Rachel's boat?" Mary Sharon asked.

"Reckon? You are completely back to being a rural girl, aren't you?" She just grinned. I turned my attention back to the boat. "Probably. We couldn't go anywhere in this wild sea anyway, but now the boat is completely useless."

"What d'ya think? Did this just happen because of the storm, or did someone purposely sabotage it?"

"Honestly? I think the storm just ripped it from its mooring and then, once it drifted out of the bay, it got smashed up here, maybe even got smashed against the shore several times before lodging here."

"You're probably right. But still. Awfully convenient, hmm?"

When we turned back to the path, in spite of the crashing of the waves, we heard a loud rustling and snapping of twigs. We both froze as Aggie took a step or two, growling. I lunged forward, grabbing her collar. Neither Mary Sharon nor I were breathing, I realized. "Breathe," I ordered quietly, then said loudly, "Who's there?"

The only response was more noise. Aggie started barking frantically. There was a lot of racket now, and I saw the blur of a deer moving away from us. In my relief, I loosened my hold on Aggie, and she slipped out of my grasp and charged into the woods. "Aggie!" I shouted, to no avail. "Oh, damn. Aggie?" She kept barking and chasing for a few more minutes before rejoining us and shaking moisture all over.

"Thanks, Aggie," Mary Sharon tried to step away. To me, she merely raised her eyebrows.

"Didn't you see it? It was a deer."

"You actually saw a deer? Or are you just guessing?"

"No, no, I actually saw it. Just a glimpse."

"You're sure?"

Now I was starting to doubt my own eyes, wondering if I'd conjured up a vision of a deer. "I think so. No, I'm sure. Really. It was a deer."

We continued our walk. Staying as close to the water as we could, we pretty much circled the island without finding anything else. Back at the cabin, I said, "Of course, there's still the interior of the island." Mary Sharon nodded, and we went inside.

"**W**here have you been?" Julie demanded as we entered the cabin. "We were worried to death about you!"

"*You* were worried to death," Rachel corrected her. "Do you want some coffee or hot chocolate?" she asked us.

"Coffee, thanks," I answered while Mary Sharon asked for hot chocolate.

"Find anything out there?"

"What kind of animals are on this island?" Mary Sharon asked, instead of answering her question.

Rachel raised her eyebrows. "Animals? The usual, I guess. Fox, deer, racoon, chipmunks, squirrels, like that. Birds, of course. Why?"

"We heard some noise in the woods and just wondered what made it, that's all."

I frowned. "We *know* what made it, Mary Sharon. I told you it was a deer." To Rachel, I said, "She just wanted to make sure there *were* deer on the island, that I wasn't just making it up."

Everyone was gathered around the fire again, which Grace was stirring. The wind seemed to be rising, rain spattered the windows.

"Phone still not work?" I asked. Rachel shook her head, picked it up and tried it once more, then shook her head again. "I think we found the boat, Rachel. Is it called the Carolina?" I'd noted the name on the hull when we were examining it.

"Yes, after my grandmother."

"Is it okay? Can we get out of here?" Julie asked.

I shook my head. "Julie, the sea is too dangerous for us to go anywhere anyway, but—no, it's not okay. It was smashed against the rocks, completely disabled."

There was a collective sucking in of breath before Teddie asked, "Do you think it was deliberate?"

I spread my hands and shook my head. "It's impossible to say for sure. My guess is that the storm just took it and smashed it up. But—I could be wrong."

"Find anything else out there?" Grace asked.

I shook my head, and Mary Sharon answered, "No, but mind you, we didn't do an exhaustive examination of the island."

Julie inquired, "So Grace, are you going to tell us about this client of yours?"

This time Grace just stared at Julie with steady eyes. "There's nothing to tell. I've thought about it all morning. I haven't seen him since April of last year, about fourteen months ago. That's it."

"Was your relationship with him a cordial one, a good one?" Julie persisted.

"Julie. He was a *client.* I did *not* have a 'relationship' with him. Our dealings were . . . less than cordial."

"I think you'd better tell us about these 'less than cordial' dealings in detail."

"Well, Julie, you can 'think' that all you want. I have no intention of discussing it with you."

"Grace! This is a *murder* investigation!"

"And *you* are not the police."

Julie appealed to the rest of us, but none of us would back her up. She made a clicking noise with her tongue and said, "At least tell us whether or not you have a gun, Grace."

"Here?" Grace asked, and when Julie nodded, she said, "No. Do you?"

When Julie looked uncomfortable but didn't answer, Teddie pressed her. "Julie. *Do* you have a gun?"

Julie rolled her shoulders a little and said, "Yes, but I haven't taken it out or anything. It's still in my purse."

"What?" Rachel exclaimed.

"Why do you have a gun?" Mary Sharon asked.

"Tony—my husband—gave it to me," she said defensively. "I work downtown, not always the safest place, so he just wanted me to have some protection."

"Why would you bring it here?" Rachel asked.

"Oh, I just forgot it was in there," Julie answered, then immediately contradicted herself. "Anyway, Tony thought I should bring it. You never know . . ."

"Does anyone else have a gun? Here?" Rachel looked around at our faces, and we all shook our heads.

With an edge to her voice, Teddie said, "I live in probably the most dangerous city in the world, and I don't *own* a gun. What does that mean, Julie, 'not the safest place?' Where do you live these days? One of those lily-white suburbs?" She didn't wait for Julie's answer. "A lot of people of color downtown, are there?"

Julie squirmed and looked embarrassed. "That's not what I meant, Teddie."

"Uh-huh," Teddie said angrily as she got up to slam a piece of wood into the fire, sparks flying far enough that Grace jumped to avoid them. She turned back toward Julie, her eyes mirroring the stormy skies outside and said with a low voice, "What happened to you, Girl? You give up all your politics when you gave up women?"

"Teddie," Julie cajoled, "it's not like that. Really . . ." Again she appealed to the rest of us, but we remained silent.

After a moment, Rachel said, "Julie, I think you'd better bring that gun here."

"You think *I* killed that man?" Julie erupted. "I don't even know him!"

"I don't think *any* of us killed him," Rachel said with a steeliness to her voice. "But if there's going to be a gun in *my* house, I want to know where it is."

"Okay," Julie acquiesced and went upstairs.

We all stared into the fire or out the window, avoiding eye contact. Mary Sharon finally broke the silence and said, "Just because she might be a little racist—my god, you don't think she votes Republican, do you?—doesn't mean she's a murderer."

There was a little whoosh of exhaled breath as we chuckled, and Grace said, "You're probably right. Anyway, she might be a Perot fan instead of a Republican." This time we groaned in unison, after which Grace continued, "She *does* do sexual harassment law, after all. She can't be all bad."

Rachel was looking at Teddie carefully when she said, "It's an awful disappointment, but Grace is right, we should probably cut her a little slack. You know, not everyone is as perfect as *we* are." Grinning, we all murmured agreement and stopped talking when we heard Julie's footsteps on the stairs.

She came into the room with a large, white, plastic purse—a bag I would never be caught dead with. I wondered, idly, how someone really could change that much. Or maybe she hadn't. Maybe she'd just reverted to her true self. *Who is our true self, though?* I wondered. *That person our parents and society tried to mold us into? The one we discovered in rebellion against that early training? A combination of these things?* I shook my head to clear it of this meandering.

Julie looked distinctly upset. "It's gone," she said in a tiny voice.

"Gone?" Rachel asked.

"What do you mean, 'gone?'" Mary Sharon pursued.

"Julie," I added my voice, "what are you saying?"

She spoke louder as she dumped the stuff in her purse out on the coffee table. "It's gone, I'm saying. Gone. It's not in my purse anymore. See?" She showed us a little pocket inside the purse. "This is where I keep it, and there's nothing there now!"

We stared at the array of stuff on the table—a makeup bag, a notebook, a pill box, pens, nail files, a small container of tissues, a glasses case, a wallet, an address book, keys, a booklet of photos, a paperback copy of a Jane Smiley book. But no gun.

No one knew what to say, I guess, so we didn't say anything—we just continued to stare dumbly at the pile of stuff on the coffee table. I glanced at Mary Sharon, who lifted an eyebrow in return. A missing gun, missing from a purse that had been in this house the past twenty hours, made this crime seem closer to home. It seemed as though one of us—I carefully raised my eyes without moving my head, to look at the five others; no one was looking back at me or at each other—had to have taken the gun. Or else Julie herself . . . Either of which meant . . .

"This is stupid! I must have forgotten it at home. I'll just call Tony and . . ." Her voice drifted off, as she realized, of course, that she couldn't call anyone.

Rachel grabbed the phone and pushed the "on" button, then shook her head again. "Julie, did you tell anyone you had a gun in your purse?"

Julie furrowed her brow and shook her head. "No. I'm sure I didn't. I . . ." She looked around at us helplessly. "I know you guys. I knew you'd disapprove. I wouldn't have told you. I *must* have forgotten it," she repeated.

"But you don't really think you did, do you?" Mary Sharon inquired. Julie shook her head.

"If you brought the gun, and you didn't tell any of us about its existence, then *you* must've used it and disposed of it yourself," Teddie said crisply.

"I didn't! Come on! I don't know that guy. Why would I kill someone I don't even know?"

"Maybe you did know him," Grace said quietly.

Julie shook her head. "This is ridiculous! If I had brought a gun here and shot someone with it, I wouldn't have told you I had it. I mean, why would I tell you? All I had to do was say the same thing all of you said. 'No, I don't have a gun.' Why would I tell you I did if I knew it was missing?"

"She's got a point," I agreed, and Julie glanced at me gratefully.

"But then what?" Rachel asked. "If we didn't know it was here, we wouldn't think of looking for it, would we? And it seems quite inconceivable that someone from outside the cabin managed to get in here and find a gun. Julie, where has your purse been since you arrived?"

Julie gnawed on her lower lip, thinking for a minute. "It's hard to remember exactly because I was so sick when I got here. I guess I dropped everything just inside the door and made for the bathroom. It stayed there until we went to bed. I took my purse upstairs with my suitcase, and it's been in my room ever since."

Teddie nodded. "Yeah, that makes sense. All of our stuff was in a heap by the back door. And I remember seeing that purse in our bedroom last night."

"So anyone going to the bathroom or kitchen alone might have gone through that stuff and found the gun," Grace said.

"But why would they?" Mary Sharon asked.

Grace shrugged and said, "Maybe they were looking for something else?"

"And," Julie said, her spirits rising a little, "someone might have just opened the back door and gone through things." We frowned in disbelief at this suggestion. "Well, they might have!" she insisted. "That door wasn't locked until after Teddie saw the guy outside, was it, Rachel?"

"No, it wasn't. I usually never lock the doors here," Rachel added. "What would be the point?"

"Especially in a violent storm," Grace agreed.

"Anyway," Mary Sharon said, "I can't picture anyone, inside or outside this house, going through that stuff in the back hall. It would've been too risky, too easy for any of us to catch them." Most of us nodded agreement.

We stared, again, at the jumble of stuff from Julie's purse. Finally, I said, "Julie, was this gun loaded?"

She nodded miserably. "Of course. What good would it be to carry an unloaded gun?"

What good, indeed? And then another thought occurred to me. "Wait a minute. Julie. How could you have gotten through the metal detectors at the airport with a gun in your purse?"

"Yeah!" Teddie pounced.

A long silence ensued while we all stared at Julie, and she stared at her lap. She finally sucked in a deep breath and said, "Okay. I didn't actually *forget* that I had the gun. I took it out of my purse at home and put it in my suitcase."

"Why did you bring a gun here?" Rachel asked the question again.

Julie shrugged uncomfortably. "I don't know. I'm just used to it, I guess. And . . . it's kind of wild here, with animals and stuff. I was just being cautious. Tony said . . ." she hesitated, "he said he'd never go in the woods unarmed."

"So." Grace stared at Julie. "Why are we looking in your purse? Is the gun still in your suitcase?"

"No! That's the point. When I moved my stuff upstairs last night, and Teddie was using the bathroom, I took the gun out of my suitcase and put it in my purse. Now . . . it's gone."

"This makes even less sense!" Mary Sharon burst out. "You had the gun upstairs when you went to bed. You saw it, right?"

"Yes! I took it out and put it in this little pocket in my purse." She indicated the pocket again.

"So, how could anyone have gotten it then? Unless . . ."

"Unless I used it myself?"

"Or I did, I suppose," Teddie said, quieter.

Mary Sharon nodded but said nothing more. After a moment, Rachel said, "Or Julie's lying about this, too, and the gun is just secreted somewhere else." Julie's face was stony, but she said nothing. After a moment, Rachel added, "Is anything else missing, Julie?"

She poked through her things, opening the wallet and riffling through her credit cards and cash. "I don't think so. It looks like everything is here."

"Maybe we all ought to check our things," I suggested. This was met with sullen resistance. As we rose to go to our rooms, a clap of thunder bellowed so loudly it sounded like a gunshot. We ducked, yelping a little.

"Oh, my god! My heart is just pounding like a freight train in my chest!" Teddie exclaimed, and we all patted our hearts in agreement as the skies opened up and another deluge began, scattered thunder rumbling and lightning brightening the dark sky.

"Here we go again. This really *is* like being in a mystery book. Do you have any idea how unusual it is for one, let alone two, lightning storms to occur in this area?" Grace said, moving to the windows. We knew it was a rhetorical question. Rachel checked the phone again.

Then we all headed to our rooms to go through our things. After a short while, we reconvened in the living room. Teddie added more wood to the fire and stirred it. No one had found anything missing.

"You're sure, Julie, that you told no one about bringing a gun?" Mary Sharon asked again.

"I'm sure."

I changed the subject. "Rachel, what day did you and Grace say you got here?"

"Wednesday."

"And this is Saturday. So you were here part of Wednesday, all day Thursday," I winced at a loud crack of thunder, "and part of Friday before the rest of us arrived." Rachel nodded, and I turned to Grace, who also nodded. "Did you ramble around the island any?"

They looked at each other and shook their heads. "Not really," Grace said. "I took that one path—well, maybe you don't know them yet—but I took a path out front that leads to a cliff. And back again. That was the extent of my 'rambling.' I spent most of my time on the couch or helping Rachel."

"You were helping me? Now how come I don't remember that?" Grace made a face at her. "I didn't roam around at all. I was too busy cooking and cleaning and getting everything ready. Why are you asking this, Tyler?"

"I'm just wondering if someone was *already* on the island. That would make more sense than the thought of someone landing here after that storm started." As if to punctuate my words, another loud crash of thunder occurred. "I wish we could get out there and check things more carefully." I looked at the windows being lashed by rain and wind again.

"I wish we could just get out of here," Julie said in a tight, miserable voice.

"*I* wish we could reach the cops and get some professionals in here," Teddie said.

"What if . . ." I started, then hesitated.

"What?" Grace prodded.

I sighed. "What if this guy—what's his name, Grace?"

Something in her face closed down, but she said, "I don't remember. Blake something, I think. Or maybe that was his last name."

I didn't believe her; I don't think any of us believed her, but I let it pass, not being able to think of any way I could make her tell me his whole name. *But why?* I wondered. *Why is she holding this back?* "What if this Blake fella was shot before we even arrived? I mean, Rachel, are you sure the body was completely fresh?"

She looked surprised, then considered. "No, I'm not. I didn't really check it that carefully. At any rate, it would have been hard to check because of the rain, and the temperature of the body would've been affected by that. Rigor mortis was setting in, but that tells us the least amount of time that's elapsed, not the most. Of course, he hadn't been there *very* long. The weather and . . ." she hesitated, "animals would have set upon him."

"Could it have been there before you two arrived?" I asked.

"You mean dead? His body?" I nodded. "No, I don't think so. More damage would have been done to the body if it had been lying there for two days. Maybe as long as twenty-four hours, but even that would be pushing it."

"Except," Grace interrupted, "there was no storm, no thunder, before you all arrived."

"So?"

"This island isn't that big, Tyler. How could someone have shot someone without our hearing?"

I grimaced. "Unless they had a silencer?"

"Somehow that doesn't seem likely in the woods. Although I guess it's possible."

After a few moments' silence, Mary Sharon asked, "You know what this reminds me of?"

"Oh, no. Does she still do this?" Teddie asked.

I grinned. "Oh yeah, she still does this. Let me guess, Mary Sharon. Johnny Callahan's suicide?"

She frowned. "No. But that might've worked, Tyler, and if I *was* going to use it to make a point, you would've ruined the story by giving that much of it away."

"Sorry," I said, insincerely.

"Uh-huh, I can tell."

"Let me try," Grace interrupted. "How about the Landvik twins?"

"My god, Grace!" Mary Sharon stared at her. "You remember the Landvik twins? I thought you were always too stoned to hear any of my stories."

"Mary Sharon," Grace said dryly, "you forget. This motley crew of friends made me, no *forced* me, just because they were having *sexual* dalliances with one another, to spend two friggin' years in a sunroom with you and your friggin' Stone Mountain . . ."

"Rocky Ridge," Mary Sharon corrected her.

". . . Rocky Ridge/Stone Mountain/whatever stories. I swear, I know every family in that friggin' town. I could walk right up to Betty Welliver and say, 'Hey Betty, that son of yours out of prison yet, or did they just get him for something else?'"

"Oh, my god. You really were listening, Grace. I love it!" And Mary Sharon threw her arms around Grace and hugged her.

Grace retreated, as she usually did from physical contact, saying, "Okay, okay. For christ's sake, Mary Sharon. There's not enough pot in the world to drown out a hometown girl like you!"

By this time, we were all laughing.

"**S**o?" Rachel said. "Are we going to hear the story or aren't we, Mary Sharon?"

Mary Sharon smiled. "Of course you're going to hear it. This is about Letitia Nelson. Lots of Nelsons in our town, most of them related to one another. Now Letitia was a fine woman. Even though she refused to go to church. Ever since her baby boy, Eli Elmer Nelson, died at only eleven months old, she'd refused to go to church. 'If'n there were a God in heaven,' she insisted, 'then baby Eli Elmer would still be alive. I don't believe there *is* a God, so there's no point in my going to a place to worship a nonbeing.' Her logic was unassailable, so no one really argued with her. And it was clear, anyway, that she was a fine woman—a moral and upright woman—even though she did refuse to go to church.

"Letitia worked at the Ben Franklin in town. A kind of small general store, for those of you who don't know about such things." *As if,* I thought, *after years of hearing Mary Sharon's hometown stories, any of us didn't know what a Ben Franklin was.* I smiled, thinking about how well Mary Sharon probably fit in where she lived now, as Grand Marais also had a Ben Franklin. "Once baby Eli Elmer died, she quit church and got this job, never had any more kids, and never looked back. After her husband died, she just kept working until she died, twenty some years later. When I was a kid, in the '50s and '60s, it seemed like she was already as old as dirt. And she didn't die until 1979!

"Anyway. One day someone gave her a fifty-dollar bill for a purchase. Large bills like that were pretty unusual, so she wasn't likely to forget it. She made change for the person, then tucked the bill under the cash register drawer where checks and bills larger than twenty always got put, and thought nothing more of it.

"At the end of the day, when she was balancing the day's receipts, that fifty-dollar bill was not in the register. Now, first you have to know that there were only three people in the store ever allowed in this cash register: Letitia herself; George Hiram, the owner of the store; and the other woman who worked the counter, Elsie Jarl. There was only one other employee, and that was an after-school stock boy, at the time one Gary Keller, but he was never allowed to have *anything* to do with the cash register. And only Letitia and George ever balanced the receipts. One or the other of them always stayed after closing to do this. Then whoever did this would put the cash and checks in the safe in George's office in the back of the store, the opposite one checking the work the next morning and walking the money over to the bank two doors down.

"But naturally, Letitia remembered that fifty-dollar bill, and it wasn't there. She lifted the cash register drawer up to see if the bill was stuck somehow to the bottom of the drawer. She went through all the money and checks in the piles on the counters to make sure the bill wasn't just plastered against another bill or check, and she'd missed it. Actually, she did this about three times. Then she checked every piece of the counter itself: under the cash register, in the two drawers under the counter, on the shelves beneath the drawers, every square inch of that area. She even got down on her hands and knees and looked under the counter and all around it. That fifty-dollar bill had just plumb disappeared.

"She then thought that maybe it had gotten used for change, although she couldn't imagine anyone making such a large purchase that they'd get fifty or more dollars back in change, but she went ahead and rung out to see if maybe everything actually balanced anyway. It didn't. She was fifty dollars short. So now she was feeling pretty desperate. She repeated all her attempts to find the bill again, to no avail. Then she had a brainstorm. She thought maybe George had seen that fifty-dollar bill and put it, already, for safekeeping in his safe. She virtually flew back to George's office and was mightily disappointed when it wasn't there."

Mary Sharon paused for a minute, getting up to stir the fire and put another log on. The wind, howling around the corners of the cabin, was competing with the pounding rain. She looked out the window for a minute at the wild storm. We all grinned at one another, stretched a little, knowing she'd return to her seat and her story.

"Elsie, by then," Mary Sharon resumed, "was just putting on her hat to go home. George had already left, it being Letitia's turn to close up. And Gary had just left, too. 'Elsie,' Letitia asked her, 'did you see a fifty-dollar bill in the till today?' But Elsie couldn't remember. She wasn't terribly observant, so this didn't exactly surprise Letitia. After Elsie left, Letitia again checked every possible place once more, including her dress and slip, on the off-chance that it had just clung to her when she went to put it away. She checked the wastebasket by the front counter, then eventually all the wastebaskets, and most of the store.

"She finally had to concede defeat and call George at home. He just told his wife, 'Problem at the store,' and hurried on down. Letitia and George spent the next couple of hours tearing that store apart. And never finding the money. In the '60s, fifty dollars was a lot of money. Letitia, the model of serene comportment, was feeling frazzled and frayed. She knew *she* hadn't taken that money, but she also knew that, sooner or later, George would have to wonder. He finally threw in the towel and told Letitia to go home. He said he'd stop at Elsie's and Gary's on his way home to question them, but they would just have to wait until morning to see if the money turned up and decide what to do then, if it didn't.

"Letitia went home and made herself something to eat but ate it with no memory of having done so and went to bed and probably slept, also with no memory of having done so. She kept turning over in her mind every possible scenario she could come up with to imagine what might have happened to that fifty-dollar bill. She knew that she could and would just take responsibility for its loss and give the store fifty dollars of her own to make up for her carelessness, but she also knew that George would then be faced with the dilemma of wondering if she'd tried to steal it or if she was just plain dumb and/or careless and should he let her go?"

At this point, Mary Sharon got up and darted into the kitchen. "Whew. I'm hungry," she said.

"Mary Sharon!" Teddie snapped, and we all echoed her protest.

"I'll be right back," came the muffled reply from behind a refrigerator door.

We all grinned at one another and shook our heads. This was a Mary Sharon technique: keep them hanging.

"Well, I'm going to get something to eat, too," Teddie declared and followed Mary Sharon to the kitchen. Shortly, there was an array of sandwich fixings spread out on the table with side plates of fruit and vegies. When we all finally settled back down with something or other to eat, Teddie demanded querulously, "Are you going to finish this damn story or aren't you, Mary Sharon?"

"Oh sure," Mary Sharon agreed equably, as if she hadn't even noticed we were all waiting impatiently. "The next morning, Letitia went in to the store prepared to throw herself, as it were, on the sacrificial fire. She'd examined every possibility and really didn't believe that either Gary or Elsie would have taken the money and knew that she hadn't, so . . . When she began to tell George how she fully intended to make good her carelessness, he brushed her away, saying, 'Oh, Letitia. I should have called you last night. There's no mystery after all. Mae,' that was his wife, 'came into the store in the early afternoon. You were busy with a customer, and I guess Elsie was in the back or something, and I'd just stepped over to see Bruce at the bank. She needed some money for groceries, so she opened the till and took that fifty dollars. She meant to tell me last night at dinner, but I flew out of there after your phone call, and she didn't get a chance to tell me until I got home later. I'm sorry. I hope you haven't been too distressed.' 'Oh, no sir,' Letitia answered, 'I'm just glad it's all settled.' And that was that."

After a slight pause, Grace added, "At least 'that was that' until they discovered Mae's body, hacked to tiny pieces behind the bank, and no one ever suspected mild-mannered Letitia Nelson of such a horrendous crime." We all laughed.

"So Mary Sharon," I asked, "are we to assume that one of us has a partner who borrowed Julie's gun for some good reason, and consequently, we should just not worry?"

Mary Sharon's eyes narrowed as she stared at me. "You know, Tyler, I'm never sure how it is you're able to write. You have such an unimaginative mind." I smiled my "idiot" smile to reassure her. "I think the point of the story is that we can fret and fret and sometimes—you just have to let go and wait for things to clear up on their own."

She was probably right, but a missing gun—a missing *loaded* gun—felt a bit more ominous than a missing fifty-dollar bill.

What Mary Sharon's story *did* do was give us permission to stop attempting to solve anything and just relax for awhile. The wind had dropped, and the thunder and lightning had quit; the rain was still coming down but now in a steady drizzle rather than giant bucketfuls. I borrowed Rachel's slicker again.

I felt a shiver of apprehension at the door and went back into the living room. "I have to take Aggie out," I announced. "Uh, anyone willing to go with?"

"I'll go with," Julie said, unfolding herself from the corner of the couch. *If any of us did this,* I thought fleetingly, *am I safer alone?*

I hadn't realized, until I got outside and took great breaths of cool, fresh air into my lungs, how smoky, overheated, and close the interior of the cabin had become, probably exacerbated by the presence of six inquisitive, suspicious minds. Aggie and Julie and I struck off on a path more or less straight through the middle of the woods. At first we just walked, not talking at all. It was soothing— our silence, the weeping of the trees, the soft plop of our feet on the spongy path.

I tried to put the puzzles of the murder—Grace's familiarity with the victim and Julie's missing gun and how all these things might connect with one another—out of my mind and just focus on my body in this place: the woods, the rain, the chilly air, the rustling in the underbrush—walking in my body, instead of in my mind. It got easier each minute I did it, but I had to continuously guard against slipping back into that cerebral life in which I so comfortably resided.

Aggie had no such struggle. She scampered ahead on the trail, stopping occasionally to look back, checking our more sedate progress. She made brief detours off the path, crashing through the brush after some imagined or actual creature or sniffing intently, deeply, and with total abandon. She lived, in ways I knew I would never accomplish, totally in the moment.

At the end of this path, we broke from the woods onto a rocky point. I'd almost forgotten that Julie was with me. I tried to calculate in what direction we'd been moving, so that I might imagine what view we would have if it weren't for the fog and low sky, but I was totally disoriented and couldn't do it. There was a makeshift bench, a couple of boards over two fat logs, that invited me, in spite of its wetness, to sit, so I did. Gazing into a misty nothingness, I decided, had its own charm.

Aggie plopped next to me, leaning slightly against my leg, her tongue out. I ruffled the damp fur on her head and scratched her ears, thinking how she was getting old, before quickly veering away from that thought. I continued to resist the temptation to sort things out and just tried to make my mind a blank, drifting in the shifting fog.

After a minute, Julie sat next to me on the bench. We said nothing for awhile. Just breathed. Then I said, quietly, "Was it so awful with women? With me?"

There was a little catch in Julie's breath, and she turned toward me. "Oh, Tyler. It's not that simple. I'm not like you. You know that. I wanted . . ."

When she hesitated, I interjected, "The security of an acceptable life? Husband, kids, station wagon, picket fence?"

"Don't make fun of me, Tyler. It's not fair." She took off her glasses, splattered with drops of moisture, and wiped them absentmindedly on her jacket.

"I'm sorry." She was right.

"Yes, I did want those things. I never wanted to swim upstream like the rest of you. I believe in feminism, I believe in all the same things you do. I just want to fight from within. And," she quickly raised her hand, "spare me your lecture on co-optation. You're probably right, but it doesn't mean I can't accomplish some good from that position, too."

"So you really love this guy? Your husband?"

She sighed, not answering for a couple of minutes. "Yes, but you know something? You were the 'love of my life,' too, Tyler. I don't think . . . I feel disloyal to Tony saying this, but I don't think I could ever be as close to *any* man as I can a woman. But. This works better for me. And much as I loved you? We were wrong for each other, Tyler. You must know that, too."

I felt a sharp ache in my throat. I didn't respond right away, bent over Aggie's head instead, trying to stanch the tears trying to escape.

"Tyler?" Julie finally said, softly.

I snapped my head up, hoping the rain would camouflage my tears, and said, "Yeah. You're right, Julie. We were . . . well, we had lots of problems, didn't we? I know I was pretty brutal to you at times. I'm sorry."

Her own eyes filled with tears. "And I'm sorry I left you in the cowardly way I did, Tyler. It was unforgivable of me."

A little bubble of a sob snuck out through my lips, and a similar sound erupted from her mouth, and we ended up with our arms around each other, bawling. I felt both embarrassed and relieved.

Finally I quit and, finding I had no tissue, pulled a leaf off a madrona tree and used it to blow my nose. I pulled another one off and offered it to Julie. We stared then, wordlessly, into the grey nothingness, our shoulders barely touching, yet still supporting one another. Finally I said, "Is this why you came this weekend?"

"Partly. You?"

"Well, I wanted to see everyone, but . . . yes, I guess I did hope this would get settled. Somehow."

She nodded, and we recommenced our gazing, and when I felt I'd almost gotten the hang of not thinking too much, we headed back the way we'd come. We ended up behind the cabin. Teddie, in a bright blue windbreaker, was out on the end of the dock. She was leaning over the edge, as if she were looking at or listening for something. For one brief second, I wondered if she was having a rendezvous with someone in a boat. Then she turned, saw us, and waved, a flash of white in her dark face indicating a smile. I waved back and made my way down the path to her. I didn't realize until I reached the dock that Julie was no longer behind me. I looked back up the hill, shrugged, and assumed she'd decided to go inside.

"Getting all wet?" I asked Teddie.

"Yeah. I just had to get out of there, you know?" I nodded. We fell into an easy rhythm, walking side by side on a path circling the edge of the bay, my long legs slowing for her shorter ones. She said, "So. You have a nice visit with your old honeypie?"

I clicked my tongue against my teeth, "Yeah." I nodded and repeated, "Yeah. It was real nice."

"Good. You cured?"

I laughed. "Yeah, Teddie, I think I am."

"'Bout time, Girlfriend, 'bout time."

"Mmmm," I agreed, feeling the old warmth of our easy connection.

"She wasn't right for you anyhow."

I smiled. "No. Nor was I for her."

"Huh," Teddie huffed a little. "No, I guess not." We smiled and linked arms. After a few minutes, she asked, "What do you make of all this, Tyler?"

"I don't know. I can't make heads or tails of it."

"It can't be a coincidence that Grace knows this fella, do you think?"

"No, I doubt it. But . . . how did he get here? And why? If he came to hurt Grace, and she—let's say—killed him to protect herself, where is his boat?"

"Maybe she let the boat loose after killing him?"

"Yeah, I guess that's possible. Or maybe two of them came, this Blake and somebody else. Then this other person killed Blake and took off in the boat."

Teddie shrugged. "That's possible, I guess. But why here? In this weather especially? And how does Julie's gun fit into all this?"

I shook my head. "I don't know. It just defies sense, doesn't it?"

Teddie nodded. We'd made it back to the cabin by then. I had gotten so wet that I needed to change into dry clothes before joining the others. When I came down, Mary Sharon was in the kitchen, stirring something in a bowl.

"What are you doing?" I asked her.

"Oh, my mother's taken over my body, I think. I'm making cookies."

"Great!" I stuck my finger in the dough, and Mary Sharon swatted it with her wooden spoon. "I like your mother's solutions."

In the living room, Rachel and Teddie were setting up a Scrabble board in front of the fire. "Want to join us?" Teddie asked.

"Don't ask her!" Rachel objected. "She'll bury us."

I smiled and held up Alix Kates Shulman's *Drinking the Rain*. "No, thanks. I want to read for awhile."

"Oh, god," Rachel groaned. "That book is so exquisitely written! Don't you just love it?"

"Yes," I agreed. Julie had curled up in one of the chairs with a book also. "Where's Grace?"

"Napping."

I nodded, thinking that sounded good, too, and plopped myself in the other chair by the fire, quickly moving into a state that vacillated between reading and dozing.

Eventually, my book slipped to the floor with a resounding crack, which brought me awake. I had been dreaming about a body drifting in the fog and awoke feeling disoriented. Everyone chuckled. I stared at the book on the floor for a moment before realizing what had happened. "Oh. I guess I fell asleep?"

"That would probably explain the snoring," Mary Sharon agreed, not taking her eyes off a book in her hands.

"Who's winning?" I asked Teddie and Rachel, still trying to clear the cobwebs out of my brain.

"She just won," Rachel said, pushing her glasses back up into her hair.

"Want to take on the champion?" Teddie was clearly talking to me.

I managed to mumble, "Maybe later."

"Tyler," Mary Sharon said. "Have a cookie. That'll wake you up."

"Good idea." I looked around the room as I munched a peanut butter cookie. Grace was sitting at the table, cards spread out in front of her, apparently playing Solitaire. Julie was still in the other chair, reading. I looked out the window. The drizzle appeared to have quit, but the sky remained dour.

"What are you reading, Mary Sharon?" Teddie asked as she rubbed Mary Sharon's feet.

Mary Sharon held up *Female Sexual Slavery* by Kathleen Barry. "Have you read this?"

"Oh yeah. Years ago."

"Me, too," Mary Sharon said. "I'm thinking of writing a book and just wanted to start reexamining all the earlier feminist treatises on this."

"What's it going to be about?" Julie asked, putting her book down.

"Prostitution. I want to update the material. But mostly, I want to reaffirm feminist analysis of the sex industry. We got derailed during the so-called 'sex wars' of the '80s, and I want to revisit the subject and get us back on track. Actually, the book would be an expansion of a long research paper I did in law school."

"Well," Julie said, "I hope you're a little kinder than those earlier feminists were."

I felt everyone in the room snap to attention at those words, and Mary Sharon said cautiously, "Kinder?"

"Well, you know," Julie seemed cautious, too, no doubt also noting the tension her words engendered. "Originally, feminists were so *judgmental* of prostitutes."

"Judgmental?" Mary Sharon queried. "I don't guess I'm exactly following your drift, Julie. I have no intention of judging prostituted women, but I certainly judge the men who prostitute them."

"'Prostituted women?'" Julie's nose wrinkled like she was encountering a new smell, but she continued without waiting for Mary Sharon to respond. "Listen. I feel like my sexuality was judged plenty when I was a lesbian. I don't think we should be judging anyone else's. *I'm* certainly never going to do that." You could hear the proverbial pin drop in the room. She looked around at us and said, "What? What incredibly *politically incorrect* thing have I said now?"

Grace stood up and came over by the fire, kind of looming over Julie. She said, in a carefully modulated yet quietly furious voice, "You think that a prostitute is exercising her *sexuality?*"

"Yes," Julie snapped. "What else would you call it? They are *adults* after all."

"So," Teddie put her oar in. "You think that prostitution is just a choice?"

"Of course," Julie snapped again. "They can get out if they don't want to do it, can't they?"

"And how," Grace continued in that same cold voice, "do you account for the fact that the average age—listen to this, Julie, A-V-E-R-A-G-E—age—for a girl to be brought into the 'life' is fourteen? Do you really think it's a 'career choice' at that age? Do you really think she's *exercising her sexuality?*" I didn't think I'd ever seen Grace like this and wondered what button Julie had pressed.

"Well, obviously, I'm not talking about *girls*," Julie responded. "That's kind of beside the point, Grace."

"No, Julie, it's not beside the point. It *is* the point. Are you deaf?" Teddie jumped in again. Mary Sharon and I glanced at each other. It felt like those "sex wars" were about to be resurrected right here. "If the average age a girl is first prostituted—and think about that, Julie, *average* means some are younger—is fourteen, and we concede that fourteen-year-old girls are not capable of career choices and cannot claim much knowledge about *their* sexuality, can't you see that choice and sexuality have little to do with prostitution?"

"I'm just saying," Julie refused to swerve from her line of thinking, "that prostitutes, *adult* prostitutes, have the right to choose their form of sexuality without those of us who *aren't* prostitutes coming in and telling them how awful it is that they do this. It's none of our business."

After a moment of silence in which I felt everyone was preparing to pounce on Julie, Mary Sharon—ever the voice of reason—said, "Look, Julie, I know you're feeling under attack here, but we're just trying to help you to see what's so obvious, I guess, to the rest of us. Prostitution is not a career choice. It is not something that women choose, it's something that is *done* to them. Like rape. Like domestic abuse. Like incest. Women are prostituted because it's a huge financial industry making many men rich. They are prostituted because we live in a rape culture, a culture that, by and large, still thinks women exist to take care of men's lives—washing their clothes, cleaning their houses, raising their children, meeting their needs—sexual and otherwise. And finally, they are prostituted because that sexuality you want to believe in has been so colonized by the male power systems in this society that it no longer exists independently from male definition."

"Well, aren't they also prostitutes because of the money? And because they like sex? At least some of them?"

"Julie, don't you know *anything* about prostitution?" Teddie demanded. "In the first place, few women *make* money being prostituted. Most of it goes to their pimps. They're lucky if they get enough to feed their drug habit—which is what makes prostitution possible for many of them. And also keeps them in the life. Sex? Prostitution is closer to *rape* than it is to sex. When you say 'they like sex,' it's the same as saying, 'why didn't you just lie back and enjoy it?' to a woman who has been raped."

"How come some adult prostitutes defend their *right* to be what they are, insist that it *is* a career choice, a feminist choice even?" Julie refused to budge.

Grace sighed loudly and said, very quietly, "How come wives, who are miserable and sometimes beaten and abused, defend their husbands and the institution of marriage?"

"And when they leave those marriages," Mary Sharon added, "the truth of their misery and pain and abuse pours out of them. Like it does prostituted women when they extract themselves from that life." She continued, earnestly, "Julie, fourteen-year-old girls, and younger girls, are being coerced, seduced, and enticed into the 'life,' usually by the promise of 'love' from very smooth, attractive older men. More often than not, these girls are runaways from desperate home situations and are already living on the streets, maybe turning a trick or two to survive. They are almost always girls who have been hurt sexually: raped by their fathers, their brothers, their neighbors. Their 'sweet-talking men'—the pimps—not only turn them over to other men, not so sweet-talking, but also shoot them up, get them hooked on drugs to ensure their cooperation. As prostituted women, they are like sexual slaves: they are raped, they are beaten, they are abused. These are the real facts of their lives, not those *Pretty Woman* movie-versions we're all subjected to. Prostitution is a form of violence against women that every feminist, every *thinking* woman, should want exposed."

Julie shook her head and said stubbornly (making me think of the Julie I fell in love with, but who also irritated me enormously), "Maybe we could just agree to disagree here? And drop the subject?"

"Nothing we've said has had any impact on you?" Teddie asked.

"Of course! I'm not the idiot you all seem to think I am! I still think . . . Oh, what's the use? You're such know-it-alls. *I'm* a feminist, too, you know. And I know plenty of feminists who think the way I do." *And live in suburbs,* I thought uncharitably, because the truth was, I knew plenty of feminists (even those who *didn't* live in suburbs) who thought exactly as she did, too. "Maybe we should just talk to a *real* prostitute."

Grace had her back to Julie and was staring into the fire. At those final words, she whipped around and declared fiercely, "You *are* talking to a real prostitute!"

There was absolute, stunned silence following this revelation.

Rachel finally said, "Grace?"

Grace waved her hand dismissively at her while never taking her burning eyes off of Julie. I looked at Rachel. This information was clearly not news to her. Things fell into place in my mind with a resounding thud: Rachel and Grace's bond, the suspicion of abuse in Grace's life, her father's obit, and now this.

Julie finally broke the silence with, "But . . . I thought you ran a temp agency."

Grace barked a mirthless laugh. "I do. We provide a temporary service to men."

Julie tried again. "But . . . I mean, aren't you a perfect example of what I'm trying to say?"

"What is that supposed to mean?" Grace said quietly.

Julie shrunk away from Grace's fury but persisted, "I mean. Look at you." She flipped her hand toward Grace, looked around at the rest of us for support that wasn't forthcoming. "You choose your life, don't you?"

"Do I? Is that what you think? What do you *know* about my life?" Her eyes swept over all of us. "What do any of you know about my life?"

No one responded for a few seconds, then Mary Sharon said, her voice as quiet and clear as Grace's, "Not much. No more than you've ever chosen to tell us."

"And that's my fault?" Grace uttered.

Mary Sharon shook her head. "I didn't say that, Grace."

Grace's scowl softened only slightly. "Well, I'll *share* with you now. I'll tell you all about *choice,* Julie. And I'd appreciate it if you would do me, a *real* prostitute, the courtesy of listening. I was eight the first time my father came to my room and fucked me." Her voice had taken on a cold, passionless tone that I'd found common in my interviews with abuse victims. "Do you think that was my first *sexual* experience, Julie?"

Julie frowned. "Well, I suppose it was . . ."

"You're wrong!" Grace roared, silencing her. "Dead wrong." Her voice dropped back to that lifeless tone again. "It was rape. Rape is not a *sexual* experience. It was my first experience with a power system over which I had no control. It was my first experience with helplessness. It was my first lesson in so-called *choice.* This went on for years. When I was a teenager, my father had me sterilized."

The room was filled with the sound of sucked-in breath and half-moans. Julie looked around at all of us, "Grace . . ."

"Just shut up, Julie," Rachel interrupted. "Listen to her. I'd kick you out of my house, if there was anywhere for you to go."

Grace continued as if there'd been no interruption. "He had me sterilized for obvious reasons—because he didn't want to be concerned with the possibility of pregnancy. It was much more than just him by then. He used me to finalize his business dealings. His friends adored being with this 'sweet and sexy' young woman." I couldn't prevent this scene from invading my mind, and a murderous rage twisted my gut. How did women survive this?

"But when you were at the U with us?" Julie asked carefully.

"By then I'd created my hippie self—dirty and disheveled and disgusting. At least by my father's standards. He couldn't force me to clean up. He tried, but beatings weren't very effective after what he'd already subjected me to. His friends didn't find me so attractive anymore, especially when I told them I had gonorrhea, which was true, actually."

She paused, and none of us said anything.

"But I'd discovered I had a kind of power over men. It was an illusion, but it seemed real to me then. So, even when I was living with you all, I was tricking. You assumed my money and tuition and stuff came from my father, but when I started refusing to perform for him and his buddies, he cut me off financially, assuming I'd capitulate.

"Except what I did was go into business for myself. I'll spare you the details. Also, I went to several of his old friends and blackmailed them. This is what put me through college."

Again there was silence; this time even Julie didn't interrupt with any observations. "When I moved to Seattle, I went into the 'life' fulltime. I tried to freelance, but that doesn't much work; it's a long and not-pretty story. In brief, territory is 'protected' by pimps. If you don't become a member of their 'stable,' you get hurt. Badly." With no show of emotion, she tugged at her sweater's neck, revealing a long scar running across her clavicle. "So I ended up with a pimp. By this time, I was way beyond the dope that helped me survive through my high school and college years. I was taking cocaine, crack, heroin. Anything, everything. I wanted oblivion; I'd do anything to get it.

"Finally, about ten years ago, Rachel virtually kidnapped me and got me into rehab." She raised her eyes and smiled at Rachel, who smiled back. I thought of the times when Mary Sharon had been there for me, too, and looked over at her. She caught the movement of my head and gazed back. "It's a constant struggle, *constant,* but I've been clean for eight years now."

"Nice work, Grace," I said quietly, and the others mumbled agreement. Grace's eyes flickered in my direction, and then she continued as if she hadn't noticed we'd responded. "I run a house in Seattle now. It's pretty safe. The women who work there live there. If they have children, they live there with them. They're off the streets, out from under the thumb of pimps, and they engage only in safe sex, mostly free of the constant threat of violence."

"How do you do that?" Mary Sharon asked.

"When men come to our house, they're informed that they must use a condom and that if they like it rough, they should go elsewhere. If, once in the privacy of the rooms, they refuse to use a condom and attempt to force themselves without it, or if they start to get rough in any other way, we have voice-activated alarms that respond to one word and one word only. All the women have to do is say that word and an alarm goes off. Then the rest of us, no matter what we are doing, proceed to that room and evict the guy from the premises. It works most of the time."

"*Most* of the time?"

Her eyes were bleak. "Some men know about our system, come prepared. We try to screen them, but . . . Anyway, before the woman he's with can say anything, he has gagged her, then he does things to hurt her—not just sexual things. Right now, one of our women has AIDS because a guy refused to use a condom. This isn't a safe job. Ever."

"How does it work financially?" Teddie asked.

"We all put a percentage into a pot for the house expenses and health insurance and stuff. Part of our earnings goes into another pot to finance rehab, from drug use or prostitution or both, if anyone chooses to go that route. Otherwise, we keep what we earn."

"It sounds very reasonable," Julie said carefully. "Grace, I'm confused." She looked around at the rest of us. Rachel had perched on the arm of my chair, and we were leaning against one another. "I know you all think I'm the class dunce here, but I really don't get this. I mean, here you are, Grace—gorgeous and intelligent and educated and articulate. You could do anything! And you're not using drugs anymore. So, aren't I right? In the end, it's become a choice?"

Grace sighed and stared at Julie with smoldering eyes. "You don't get it, do you, Julie? Of course, I haven't told you everything. I haven't told you how my father whispered in my ear, night after night, for years, 'This is your fault. You're evil. You *make* me do this to you. You walk by me, twitching that firm little ass of yours toward me—I know you're telling me to come get it. I would never do this if you didn't make me. You want it, I know you do. It's just part of your game to pretend that it hurts or scares you. I would never do anything to hurt or scare you. I love you. You're my little girl. If you tell anyone ever, then I'll have to tell them how you *made* me do this. Everyone will know how evil you are. Evil.' And he didn't do this to my sister, only me, reinforcing the idea that it *must* be my fault. *She* wasn't *asking* for it, but *I* was."

"But now you know what a load of crap that is, don't you?" Julie protested.

"Know it?" Grace asked in that icy, emotionless voice. "In my head, you mean? Sure I *know* it. But what difference do you think that makes? My body, my psyche, my spirit were taught to believe I was horribly bad long before I could *know* anything. His lessons, his words, are written on my bones and muscles and flesh in ways over which my mind's knowledge has no domain."

"Where was your mom during all of this?" Julie asked.

A look of pain flashed in Grace's eyes, and I realized she wasn't entirely numb. I didn't know if that was a good thing or not. "That's a story I'd rather not talk about. What you need to hear, Julie, is that every time someone like you, in the name of some sappy liberalism, says prostitutes are *exercising their choice,* are acting in consent, you are saying the equivalent of 'she wants it, she likes it.' It makes me furious! And anyway, why are you concentrating on ME? On *any* woman? Why aren't you focussing on the *men* who do this?"

"Okay, that makes sense to me, but . . ." Julie hesitated. "I know you don't want it or like it, but why do you do it then?"

There were angry mutters at this question, but Grace answered. "I do it, Julie, because I'm *so* damaged I can't do anything else. I know you can't understand that. You can't even imagine going through what I've gone through. In fact, you're not a hundred percent certain that you even *believe* all that I've told you today. And believe me, I've told you nothing, compared to the real details. But listen, Julie, *you're* the one who said we should talk to a real prostitute. Well, you *are* talking to a real prostitute, and what are you doing? Not listening, that's what. Why would you give them," she waved at the rest of us, "a hard time for 'judging' prostitutes when, in fact, they're the ones who get it: that prostitution is violence against women and part of a system that maintains the status quo for the male power system.

"I don't kid myself. Why do you kid yourself? I don't *choose* prostitution, I don't think this is an *honorable* profession or a profession at all, and I certainly don't think this is just a *variation* of sexuality. I'm doing what I've been *trained* to do since I was a child.

I choose to create a modicum of safety around myself and a handful of other women. It's the closest I can get to exercising *some* control. It's not enough, but it's all I can do. The truth is, I just run the place now. I make a living. I don't let men touch me anymore. But then, I don't much let anyone touch me. And still, in your eyes, Julie, and the eyes of women and men like you, I will *always* be a whore. And in my skin and soul and blood, I will always feel like I *am* a whore. Do you hear that ugly word, Julie? Whore? That's what *you* make me when you act as if I'm enjoying and choosing this life. But, hear this too, Julie, this is a degrading, humiliating, abusive life. It's *not* sexuality. And it's certainly *not* a career choice."

After a moment, Julie said, "Okay. I hear you," and looked down into her lap.

None of the rest of us said anything else, and Grace abruptly left. When we heard the back door close, Mary Sharon started to rise, but Rachel shook her head. "Let her go, Mary Sharon. She'll need to be alone for a while."

I looked up at Rachel, whose beautiful face seemed pinched with pain. There were tears running down my cheeks. I patted her arm, "You always knew, didn't you, Rach?"

She nodded. "Yeah. I was the only one she ever confided in over the years. Believe me, I've felt like I could've killed her father from the time I was about fifteen on."

"Were you around him a lot? Did he ever come on to you?"

She shook her head. "No. You know Grace. She never let anyone near her family."

"Will she be okay?" Mary Sharon asked. Rachel frowned. "I mean—with us. Now that it's all come out."

"As 'okay' as she'll ever be. Actually, she talked about telling you this weekend anyway. I encouraged her, but I don't know whether she really would've done it."

"Her father's obit," I said. "This is what it was all about."

Rachel nodded, and Teddie said, "What about his obit?" Rachel described it.

"Oh, Jesus," Teddie said. "Now it's in memorial requests? It's scary, you know?"

Julie said, in a very small but determined voice, "Don't *any* of you think that some women *do* make incest up?"

Rachel said angrily, "Is that what you think, Julie? That Grace is making this up?"

"No! I . . . No, I don't think *Grace* is, but really, don't you think *some* women do?"

Rachel didn't answer, her mouth in a tight, grim line. I glanced at her, then said, "Sure, Julie, some women do make it up. I'm certain everyone here knows that." There were nods. "But the vast majority don't. And the False Memory Syndrome?" I tightened my jaw for a moment, reining in my anger. "It's just a new way to get people to focus on anything but the truth of way too many girls' lives. Just a new variation of an age-old game: make the *poor men* look like the victims and the women look like hysterical liars." After a moment, I asked Rachel, "So this thing about the False Memory Syndrome in her father's obit—I assume that Grace confronted him about the abuse at some point?"

"Oh yeah. After getting clean of drugs, she wanted to have it out with him. It wasn't exactly helpful. She ended up going through treatment a second time a year later."

"And her mother backed her father up?"

Rachel nodded. "The whole family did. Treated her as if she were crazy. It's a long, devastating story. When she came back to Seattle, after the second treatment, she got an unlisted number, changed her last name, and has never talked to anyone in the family since."

"What's her name now?" Teddie asked.

"Dworkin."

"After Andrea Dworkin?" I asked. Rachel nodded, and I smiled a little.

Again Julie ventured carefully into this conversation, "So none of you think it's awful that . . . I mean, oh, that's she still doing this? Or making it possible, anyway, for other women to keep doing it?"

"Julie," I said, keeping my voice from rising, "weren't you the one who said feminists shouldn't be judgmental?"

"Yeah, but I was talking about what I perceived as choice. If she's not choosing this . . ."

Rachel leaned over, imparting additional intensity to her words, "Look, Julie, I don't want to see Grace in this life at all, even peripherally. I think, if she were completely healthy, she wouldn't be. But—I don't know if what I think of as 'completely healthy' is even an option to her. I do know that she's immeasurably healthier than she's been most of these thirty years I've known her. That's progress. Maybe there'll be more, maybe not. I don't know what I'd be like, what I'd be doing with my life, if I'd gone through what she's gone through. I just love the best in her and hope it has room to expand."

Julie didn't argue, just nodded.

After a polite and wary dinner during which no one talked much except to say, "Pass the salt, please," I sat next to Grace by the fire and said, "So, Grace, you want to tell us about this client of yours?"

"There's not much to tell, Miss Marple." Her smile flashed on quickly and then off again. "He only came to the house once. He didn't stay. He was one of those types who listen intently to our conditions, agree affably, and then proceed to attempt to beat their girl up." She looked at me then, away from the fire she'd been gazing into. "We always call ourselves 'girls.'" I nodded, and her gaze returned to the fire. "I guess these guys assume we won't discover they've beaten one of us until after, when it's too late. But this girl was able to say her code word . . ."

"What is the code word?" Teddie interrupted, sitting down across from us.

Grace shook her head. "I'm sorry, Teddie. We have an ironclad rule about never telling anyone what the words are. It's different for every room. And gets changed if it's ever used."

"Makes sense. I was just curious."

Grace continued. "So, we all converged on the room when she sounded the alarm—there's six of us—and informed this fella that he had to go. He was furious. Most of them leave sort of sheepishly, embarrassed at having gotten caught at being 'bad boys.' Some of them throw a lot of verbal invective around but leave anyway. This guy tried to take us on physically, striking out at us, yelling, and swinging. Personally, I think he'd heard about our techniques from someone and came with a fantasy of being abused and 'raped' by a whole room of us. A dominatrix fantasy, you know? We don't play those games. I put my gun to his head—yes, I do have a gun, but I didn't bring it here with me—and told him to get dressed and clear out. He did."

"That's it?" I prodded.

"That's it. Actually, I wouldn't even remember him— recognize him, I mean—from one visit, except he's rather well-known around town. We all laugh whenever we see his picture in the paper or anything."

"What do you mean, he's 'well-known'? Is he a politician or something?"

"No, he's a businessman. But environmental issues are pretty big news in this neck of the woods, you know. And he's always into it with some eco-group or other."

"Environmental issues?" I echoed. "What's his business?"

Grace hesitated before mumbling, "Lumber."

"Lumber," I repeated, turning slowly toward Rachel. "Lumber? Do *you* know this guy, Rachel?"

"Why would she know him?" Grace interrupted. "You know she has nothing to do with the family business! Even her parents don't."

"Grace," Rachel admonished, wriggling her shoulders a little. "Yeah, I know him." After a slight pause, she added, "Jordan Blake."

A little gurgle slipped out of Julie's mouth, but Mary Sharon asked, "How come you didn't tell us you knew him?"

"No one asked me," Rachel replied.

I looked from Rachel to Grace and back to Rachel. "What's going on here?"

"We didn't kill Jordan, if that's what you're asking," Rachel answered acerbically. "It just doesn't look very good. We're on this isolated island where a dead body shows up who just happens to be a man both Grace and I know. A little too coincidental, wouldn't you say, Columbo?" She tried to smile, and I nodded without smiling. "I probably wouldn't know him—after all, neither I nor my parents are involved in the company, as Grace said, except for reaping the profits, of course—but for the fact that he's rather important in the business. His father bought the northwest division from my grandfather, so the families know each other very well. From way back. In fact, years ago he made an attempt to 'woo' me. You know, tie the two great empires together through marriage." She laughed, mirthlessly.

"So, he's about our age?" Mary Sharon asked.

"A little older. He is—was—probably in his early fifties. When he came a-courtin', I was in my midtwenties, and I'm pretty sure he was about ten years older than me. This was about '78. He was pretty shocked to find out that the woman he thought was my housemate, Robin Parker, was actually my sweetie."

"You told him?" Julie asked.

"Sure. Robin and I were young and wildly radical and were out to everyone in those days." She shrugged. "Well, we're still *out* to everyone, I guess, but not so wild anymore."

"Did you ever see him after that?" I asked.

Rachel shook her head. "No. He sort of dropped communication with the family altogether. He was just an underling of some sort in the company then, but I gather he's taken over since his father retired a couple of years ago."

"Did he ever get married, do you know?"

"Yeah." Rachel looked at Grace.

"Oh yeah," Grace continued the story. "When he was about forty, he married a woman about half his age. They had a couple of kids right away. Just a year or two ago, she divorced him. He tried to get custody of the kids, and it all came out that he'd been beating her for years. Extremely scandalous. Of course, the environmentalists loved it—proved what a complete asshole he was, was their thinking." After a second, she said, "I guess, when I think about it, the divorce was just about a year ago because all that stuff came out in the papers not long after he'd been at the house."

"It sounds like you knew him, or of him, long before he visited your house," I ventured.

"Well, yeah, I did. I mean," she grinned at Rachel, "I'd heard the courting story from Rachel when it happened, so I was kind of aware of who he was and noted any stories I heard about him or anything that was in the paper, you know?"

"Do you think he could've known that you two were connected somehow?"

Grace shook her head, and Rachel echoed that motion. "Believe me, Tyler, we've talked about this, too. But I don't see how he could have known we knew each other unless . . ."

"Unless what?"

"Unless he was having us followed, which just seems too unbelievable to even consider. Grace and I have stayed in touch, you know. I come out here to the island at least once a year, and we almost always see each other then. I will admit to one or two dinners in Seattle at which he might've been present at the same restaurant without us noticing, but really, it seems too far-fetched. Mostly, when I came to town, Grace and I just came out here and spent a little time together."

"Yeah," Grace was staring out the window moodily, and her voice was huskier than usual, "this was one of the few places in the world where I really felt safe. And now . . ." She didn't finish the sentence. None of us pressed her.

After a few moments, I said, "Frankly, Rachel, what seems pretty far-fetched is that this man you both know somehow ended up dead on this island with the two of you here and, supposedly, neither of you know anything about his presence."

"I know," Rachel agreed. "Actually, there is something else." She hesitated, staring into the fire, and I glanced at Mary Sharon, who raised a single eyebrow. "About two or three months ago, I got a phone call from Jordan. Out of the blue. Well, I didn't actually talk to him; he left a message on my voice-mail. He just said something like 'Hi, Rachel. Long time no see. Give me a call, will you?'—which I didn't. I had no desire to talk to him. He left two or three messages in the next couple of weeks, all of which I ignored.

"I did call Grace, however, to get an update on him. His calls made me curious. She told me about his wife and the divorce and stuff. Then I got a letter from him, saying he'd been trying to get hold of me, and would I please respond? And would I please let him know the next time I was coming out to the island because he'd really like to get together . . . yada-yada-yada. He mentioned a business proposition that might interest me—or so he said, but no details. I just thought it was weird and kind of icky, so I tossed it, again not responding."

"And then?"

"I didn't hear from him again. I certainly had no intention of contacting him myself. I thought maybe his divorce made him think of 'old flames' or something. Not that I was an old flame, believe me, but men like that have their own fantasies, you know?"

"So he did know about the island then?"

"Oh yeah, his family uses it occasionally. My uncle is in charge of this place. If we want to use it, we ask him, and he lets us know whether or not it's available. But I can't imagine—because I didn't get back to him—how Jordan might know that I would be here at this time."

"Unless he called your uncle and asked?"

"Asked what, though? To use the place this specific weekend and then found out I was going to be here? Isn't that just a tad too coincidental?"

"Maybe he told your uncle he wanted to surprise you and asked him if he knew when you were going to be out here next? Your uncle would know that, yes?"

Rachel nodded and ran her finger across her lips. "Maybe." She shrugged. "It's possible, I guess. But why?"

I shrugged this time. "I don't know, Rachel. Why was he trying to reach you in the first place?"

"A business proposition?" Mary Sharon asked. "What kind of business proposition?" Rachel shrugged. "You have no idea?"

Rachel looked at Grace, then said, "Maybe."

"Maybe what?" I pressed.

"Maybe I have an idea."

"Rachel . . ." My voice expressed exasperation.

Rachel put her hands up in front of her. "It's just a guess. I don't really know."

"Well, what's your 'guess'?" Mary Sharon spelled me.

Rachel sighed. "Grace had heard there was a hostile takeover attempt on Blake's company. Maybe . . . maybe he wanted me to inject some fresh capital into the business, resuscitate it."

"Would you have considered such an idea?"

Rachel frowned and shook her head. "I'd never do business with a man like Jordan Blake."

"Wait a minute, Rachel," Teddie suddenly said. "When we all went out to where the body was this morning, you acted like you didn't know who that guy was. And all the time you not only *knew* who he was, but you knew that Grace knew, too. Turned over the body to see 'if any of us recognized him.' What was that all about?"

Rachel and Grace glanced at each other, then Rachel said, "It was just an act, concocted on the spot. Obviously, I did recognize him. Well, I thought I did. I hadn't seen him for years, but I was pretty sure it was him. I wanted to get Grace's confirmation and . . ."

"And what?"

"Frankly, I wanted to see how Grace was going to play it. Whether or not she was going to pretend she didn't know him. So I could get a sense of how I was . . . should play it."

After a few moment's silence, Mary Sharon said, "Maybe he did see you together at a restaurant once and, somehow, found out you were both going to be here this weekend and was bitter because of your rejection, Rachel, and your threat, Grace, and his wife's abandonment and his subsequent disgrace and . . ." Her voice trailed off as she clearly saw where her scenario was taking her.

"And," Grace finished for her, "he came out here with the intention of hurting us, and we killed him. In self-defense, of course."

Mary Sharon grimaced. "Yeah. I guess that's where I was going. So you didn't kill him?" This, I thought, was asked only in partial jest.

"We didn't kill him," Rachel firmly stated, then equivocated, "Well, let me put it this way. We didn't kill him together. I didn't kill him alone. And I'm reasonably certain Grace didn't do it."

Grace nodded concurrence. "Ditto. We didn't, I didn't, and I'm sure she didn't."

"So why was he here, and who *did* kill him?"

"And what happened to Julie's gun?"

At this point, Julie cleared her throat, obviously and self-consciously. "Well," she said, "this *is* interesting, isn't it? Because, you see, I know Jordan Blake, too. Sort of."

"What?"

"What do you mean?"

"How come you didn't tell us this before?"

Julie held her hand up to still the barrage of questions, again pushing her glasses up nervously. "I didn't tell you because I didn't *know* I knew him. I mean, I don't know him personally, but I know *of* him. I've never met him or anything, maybe I've seen pictures of him, I can't remember, but there was no way I knew him just by looking at him dead. Then when I heard Rachel, just now, say his whole name . . ."

"But *how* did you know him?" Mary Sharon got Julie back on track.

"Tony is a . . . well, we're both Greens. You know about the Green Party, right?" We all nodded. "Tony is into this environmental stuff a lot more than I am. Has been for years. I have my practice and the kids and our home and my other activities . . . Well, it's just Tony's thing. Anyway, most people who are heavily into environmental issues know Jordan Blake. This man is a real piece of work. He doesn't even try to be Mr. Nice Guy, like a lot of people in his industry do. He's right up front, redneck to the core . . ."

"Bigot," Mary Sharon interrupted.

"What?" Julie looked puzzled.

"I'm just suggesting you substitute 'bigot' or some other word for 'redneck.' It's a classist term, Julie, referring to people who work outside—laborers or farmers. People who literally have *red necks,* on account of their work. And the assumption and implication is that all outdoor working people are stupid and prejudiced and smallminded. It's classist."

"Huh," Julie grunted. "I've never heard anyone say that before. Like my dad, who was a farmer. He always had a red neck. Anyone who works in the fields or on a tractor all day does." Mary Sharon nodded. "Thanks, Mary Sharon."

"And Blake?" I prodded Julie.

"Yeah, well, he's notorious among the environmental groups, like Grace said. I've heard of him for years. Tony's actually had a run-in or two with him. Like I said, he's into this more than I am and . . . I don't know. They've locked horns. More than once. I know plenty of people who will be glad to know he's dead. Okay, so that's not a nice thing to say, but it's the truth."

After a pause, I said, "Let me see if I have this straight—so to speak. We have a dead body on this isolated, cut-off-from-the-rest-of-the-world island, one Jordan Blake. Shot in the back, it would appear. We have six women. One of them, Grace Dworkin," she grinned at me, "had an unpleasant encounter with this man in a city nearby. Unpleasant enough that he may have felt angry and/or revengeful. Another, Rachel Fineberg, also had a less than pleasant encounter with this same man some years ago, and he was trying to reach her just before she arrived here. And finally, a third member of this group of women, Julie Patterson—is that still your name, Julie?" She nodded. ". . . Julie Patterson, knows who this man is and harbors a marked hostility toward him. And this woman is also the only one, at least that we know of, who brought a gun with her to the island. Which is now missing, I might add."

"What are you saying?" Julie yelled, jumping to her feet. "That I brought my gun with the express intention of killing Jordan Blake?"

I looked directly at her and said, "Did you?"

"No!" she shouted.

I shook my head then. "I'm just trying to lay out all the facts, Julie." I looked around at all of us and said, "Any other revelations?"

Teddie sort of snorted and ran her hand back and forth over the stubble on her head. "The plot thickens, doesn't it? Well, Girlfriends, I know him—knew him, I guess—too. And he may have known Rachel and Grace were going to be here this weekend. Because of me."

We all stared at Teddie openmouthed. She twisted her own mouth to one side and shrugged. "I know. It's unbelievable, isn't it?"

"So spill, Teddie, what's the story?" I demanded.

"Okay. I've got this friend, she's a lobbyist for some eco-folks? And *she's* got these friends who are like big-time philanthropists? We do a little back-scratching once in a while. If I have some particular contact that could be helpful to her, I do what I can to bring them together. Then she finds a way to reciprocate. You know the score."

"And Blake?" Mary Sharon was getting impatient.

"Yeah, well, Blake. My friend wanted me to see him while I was out here. So I agreed . . ."

"But why?" Rachel was perturbed. "Why would someone who works for the environment want to make contact with Blake?"

Teddie twisted her mouth again. "You know, I really can't divulge the details. It's just an idea one of her groups had, and I was sort of enlisted to be the go-between. The negotiator, I guess you could say."

"But why you?" Mary Sharon prodded. "It's not as if your main focus is environmental issues. Is it?"

Teddie shook her head and grinned, almost impishly. "Mostly it was because I was going to be out here. And I'm black." When none of us responded to this, she continued, "You know, some of you white folk just can't handle pressure from us black folk. The idea—or hope, at least—was that Blake would fold in front of my blackly self."

"But why did *you* agree to do it?" I asked.

This time, Teddie pursed her lips before answering. "I told you, we scratch each other's backs. I was going to meet with some very wealthy folk who also might be a little afraid of saying no to a woman of color. Tackling Blake was my payback, shall we say, for entree to these other folk who might be willing to fund some of my pet projects. These are very private people, not people I could just connect with on my own. Lots of Microsoft millionaires out here, you know. So . . ."

"Quid pro quo," Grace finished. Teddie shrugged and nodded. "But why did you say, because of you, he might have known that Rachel and I were going to be here?"

"Well, in order to convince this man to even meet with me, I had to lay on the charm. I didn't know he *knew* any of us! So I told him I was coming out here for a reunion of college pals on an island in the San Juans. Then he wanted to know which one, and I told him it was a private island belonging to the Fineberg family.

He asked if I knew the Finebergs well, and I said 'sure' and so forth and so on. We were very chatty. And I wanted, after all, to impress him. I can't remember how much I actually told him, but I know I told him that you and I were old pals, Rachel, and that you would be here." She spread her arms, palms up, and finished, "Like I said, I had no idea he knew any of us. Of course, he told me that his dad had bought his business from the Finebergs, which made sense, after all, but I still didn't think it was a problem. Why would it be?"

There was a little silence following this. Then Mary Sharon said, "I'm still not sure I understand why you were meeting with him, Teddie. I mean, I understand that you were doing this so you could meet the people you wanted to meet, but why was an eco-lobbyist or some organization your friend represented wanting to meet with this guy who Julie and Grace and Rachel are all portraying as an asshole? A known anti-environmentalist?"

Teddie shook her head. "I'm sorry, I just can't tell you that. It was . . . a deal that they were trying to propose to him, something that might have served the needs of both sides of these issues."

"But that's ridiculous!" Julie burst out. "I can't even imagine in what way environmentalists could ever compromise with the likes of Blake!"

Teddie just smiled ruefully and shook her head again. Finally, Mary Sharon said, with a slight gleam in her eyes, "So Teddie. You haven't become a 'hit woman' in the intervening years since college, have you?" We laughed a little nervously.

Teddie grinned and said, positioning her arms as if she were cradling an assault weapon, "No, but it probably would be a great way to raise funds for the foundation, wouldn't it?" This was followed by nervous titters, which slowly trailed away.

"Well," I eventually spoke up, "have *you* got any confessions to make, Mary Sharon?"

"Me?" she squealed. "Oh, you mean about knowing Blake?" She shook her head. "Sorry. I didn't know him. Or even of him. How about you, Tyler?"

I echoed her response with a shaking motion of my own head. "No, but it sure seems weird that four of us in this room did know him. Did you meet with him already, Teddie?"

"No. I was staying in Seattle for a couple of days afterward. Meeting him—and these other folks."

"The Microsoft millionaires, right?" I asked.

"Well . . . yeah," Teddie agreed.

"What do you mean—'well . . . yeah'?" I demanded. "What's the hesitation about?"

"No! No hesitation!" Teddie protested. "I just . . . I don't actually know if they got their money from Microsoft! I mean . . . I just know they have money. And I know there's a lot of Microsoft money out here. But . . . it was just a guess. You know?"

"Teddie," Rachel said sternly. "What's going on?"

"Nothing. Nothing's going on."

"Then how come," Julie asked, "I get the feeling you're not telling us everything?"

"Because I'm not! I told you that already. I *can't* tell you everything. This friend of mine who runs this environmental organization . . ."

"Runs it?" Julie pounced. "Runs what? I thought your friend was a lobbyist."

Teddie looked blank for a minute, then said, "She is. She's a lobbyist, too. Listen," she put her hands up, "I just can't tell you about it."

"But why?" Julie persisted. "Why is it all a big secret? What's the name of this organization your friend runs?"

Teddie shook her head, saying, "I'm sorry."

Mary Sharon suddenly blurted, "Remember when that Sherman girl was raped and killed on campus?" Everyone nodded. "What did we want to do? Do you remember?"

Denise Sherman had been only twenty years old, hurrying through the underground tunnels at the "U" one night. She'd been at the library, and it was below zero outside. They hadn't found her body until the next morning; she'd been raped, and her head had been slammed against the concrete floor until she died. In one hand, a button was clutched. It turned out that the button belonged to one of the English Department's most popular professors. Eventually, he had been charged with murder in the first degree. And he got off, on a stupid technicality. Everyone knew he'd done it, but the law couldn't touch him. He didn't even lose his tenure.

"We wanted to plan the perfect murder," Rachel said quietly, her voice as rigid as steel.

"No, Rach," Teddie interrupted. "We *did* plan the perfect murder." Julie and I nodded our heads in agreement.

"We thought," Grace said, "that if the law wouldn't give us justice, then we ought to create our own justice."

"And if we planned the perfect murder, how come we didn't execute it?" Mary Sharon asked.

"Mostly because of you," I nudged her with my foot. "You started arguing against taking the law into our own hands, against our right to do this. Julie jumped in on your side, as I recall. Enough dissension was created that we argued with one another, instead of carrying out our plan."

"Christ," Grace exploded. "The lawyers!"

"So, Mary Sharon," Rachel asked, "are you bringing this up because you're wondering if one or more of us still thinks our own form of justice is allowable?"

Mary Sharon gazed solemnly at Rachel. "The thought certainly has crossed my mind." She looked around the circle at us, one by one. "It's been said that anyone, in the right circumstances, is capable of murder. I know, for a fact, all of us have seriously considered such a possibility."

"Damn right!" Teddie burst out. "It's why I don't own a gun. I assume I'd use it on someone if I had one." We all laughed a little, easing the tension.

"Seriously though," Mary Sharon asked, "Is there anyone here who thinks they *couldn't* kill someone, push come to shove?"

We squirmed, avoiding one another's eyes. I finally said, "I don't *think* I would kill anyone, but . . ." I spread my hands in a helpless gesture, "but I don't know. I sure as hell wanted to execute that smug, arrogant professor who got away with raping and killing Denise Sherman. And so . . ." I paused, then finished, "Yeah, I think I could if the circumstances were just right."

"I *know* I could," Grace said fiercely, but nothing more.

Rachel just nodded, and Julie said, "I want to say 'no way! never!' but now that I have kids, I don't know. I hope I'd never kill anyone, but . . . I might. I know I might. I mean, *Thelma and Louise?* I got that, completely, didn't all of you? I don't mean I thought it was all right that she killed him, I just mean I *got* it." Heads bobbed. "What about you, Mary Sharon?"

Mary Sharon shrugged, poking in the fire. "I don't think I would. Under any circumstances. And yet . . ." After a pause, "Do any of you believe in capital punishment?"

"No," Teddie responded, "but you know as well as anyone, Mary Sharon, when the state does homicide, the uneven hand of justice tends to fall more heavily on poor people and people of color."

Julie said, very quietly, "I don't believe in capital punishment in theory, but . . . sometimes when a crime is really brutal, when a child is involved or . . . I don't know. Sometimes I think, *he should die.* You know?"

"But really," Mary Sharon summed up, "overall we don't believe in capital punishment. And yet, most of us believe we're capable of murdering someone. Doesn't that strike you as incongruent?"

I shook my head slowly. "It's different, Mary Sharon. We're thinking—I'm assuming this is how we're all thinking—in terms of *knowing* someone hurt someone else and is getting away with it or *being right there* and having to defend ourselves or someone else."

"Yeah," Teddie agreed. "The word 'revenge' is bandied about, but—really—what we're talking about is justice. The kind that often doesn't happen in courtrooms."

"I know," Rachel said. "How could you two ever become lawyers? I mean, what would you do if you had to defend scum like that professor who violated Denise, then brutally murdered her?"

Julie said, very primly, "Everyone deserves a good defense. I'd do what I have to do. If the system isn't honored in every way, it will break down, and we'll have even less justice."

"Are you saying you think that scum should have gotten off on that stupid technicality? That that was justice?" shrilled Grace.

Julie shook her head, her eyes filling with tears, "No . . ."

Mary Sharon interrupted, "I think I'd have to excuse myself in such a case because Julie's right, everyone *does* deserve a good defense. And I'm pretty certain I couldn't give it. Not in those circumstances."

We each sat alone, then, with our thoughts. Finally, I stood up to stretch and, looking out the front windows, exclaimed, "Oh, my god!"

"**W**hat?!" Everyone jumped to their feet as if I was seeing yet another dead body when, in fact, I was just stirred by the incredible view. For the first time since we'd arrived, both the fog and low clouds had receded sufficiently enough for the vista that lay outside these windows to be visible. In twilight, the stretch of churning water reached across to another piece of land, where the sea's frothy fingers attempted to scale the high cliffs topped by densely packed trees.

"It's so-ooo beautiful, Rachel."

"It is, isn't it?"

"Is that an island or mainland over there?"

"It's another island."

"Do you ever see whales here?" Teddie asked.

"Sure," Rachel answered. "This is the Strait of Juan de Fuca. It's a virtual whale playground. In fact, this is the season. We might see some yet, if it stays clear."

"Aren't you ever tempted to just chuck it all and move here?" Mary Sharon asked dreamily.

Rachel smiled. "Nope. I love it here, but Minnesota is home. And this is—well, it's like paradise. I'm afraid it wouldn't be if I lived here all the time." After a pause, she added, "I'm not sure it even is now."

Just then, in the distance, the San Juan ferry chugged into view. "Rachel!" Julie said. "When was the last time you checked the phone?"

"Good idea," Rachel said, looking around for it. "Where is it?"

"Where did you last have it?" Mary Sharon asked as we all started searching.

"Somewhere in here." Mary Sharon was looking under the cushions of the chairs, and Rachel was checking in the kitchen. Julie and I poked around the dining end of the living room, and Grace said, heading for the back of the cabin, "Rachel, did you take it in the bathroom or bedroom?"

I was starting to feel a little uneasy when Teddie sang out, "Here it is!"

"Where was it?"

"On the floor, next to the couch by the fireplace." She flipped it on and put it to her ear, her eyes eager, then flat. She shook her head and handed it to Rachel. Again, we all turned it on and off, shook it, turned it on and off again, thumped it. Nothing.

"What are we going to do?" Julie asked.

Rachel looked over her shoulder, out the window; the ferry was almost out of sight. "This is the last ferry tonight. Tomorrow morning, if the phone still isn't working, we'll set off flares when the ferry goes by. They'll contact the Coast Guard, and we'll be rescued."

Julie jumped up and said excitedly, "Why don't we do it now?"

Rachel shook her head. "No, the ferry's almost out of sight. By the time we had the flares set up, they'd be gone; the flares would be wasted. We'll do it tomorrow. We'll be ready before the ferry's even in view."

"Aw, gee," Teddie said, "I thought it was gonna be, you know, like—'The mate was a mighty sailing man, the skipper brave and sure' . . ."

Mary Sharon piped in, "'Five passengers set sail that day'. . ."

And they both finished with, " 'For a three-hour tour, a three-hour tour.'"

"Yeah," Grace said, glumly, "except I don't remember any dead bodies on Gilligan's Isle."

"It would be a little more fun, I admit," Teddie said, "being stranded if we didn't have to worry about a corpse and a murderer."

"I know," Julie said. "It gives me the creeps to think of that guy lying out there in the woods, animals maybe chewing on him, and . . ."

"Enough," Mary Sharon held her hand up.

"Well, I need to stretch my legs and let Aggie stretch hers, too. Anyone want to join me?" I asked.

"I'll go," Rachel said.

She pulled on a sweater and left her glasses on the counter in the kitchen, and I put on my jacket; Aggie was very pleased to be outside again. She forged ahead as Rachel and I ambled along a new path. We didn't talk. When we came out of the woods at the end of this path, we were looking across a huge expanse of unbroken sea to a mountain range. There was a faint hint of sun peering through the violet and peach clouds.

"I bet this is sensational on clear days," I said. "That's the Olympic Peninsula, right?"

"Uh-huh," Rachel agreed. "It is an incredible vantage point. Especially for sunsets."

We sat down on a damp pile of rocks and gazed at the sky. "So did Grace's story just blow you away?" Rachel asked without looking away from the sky.

"Yes and no. I mean, I'd always suspected that she'd been abused. That was the only reasonable explanation for her commitment to asexuality and her odd ways back in college. And when you sent me her dad's obit, well I figured that was your message. Did she know you sent that out?"

"No, I just sent it to you and Mary Sharon. I knew you two would get it. But I hadn't seen Julie in all those years, and I guess I probably should've figured that Teddie would understand it, too, but I hadn't talked to her for a long time."

"God, I'm glad you didn't send it to Julie. Can you imagine?"

"Too well. As it is, I'm not sure that Julie really believes all of it. And believe me, Grace's not telling half the story."

"I believe it."

"And Julie's just the type . . ." she hesitated. "Maybe this is unfair, but I bet I'm right. She's just the type to say she knows a woman who accused her parents of atrocities and later it all came out that she'd just made it up, with the help of an obsessed therapist. You know?"

"Oh yeah. Exactly what I was thinking. She probably thinks the False Memory Syndrome is essential to protect poor hapless relatives from raving lunatics who . . . Well. You know the drill."

"Yes, I do know the drill. And then some. I'd like people to see some of the kids I have to treat. Some of the little girls have syphilis at four! At four, Tyler! Well, you know, you went through all of this when you did the interviews for your book, didn't you?" I nodded. "It was a terrific book, Tyler."

"Thanks. I really appreciate that, coming from you. I admire the way you live your life so much, Rachel."

"Thank you. You don't do so bad yourself." We smiled at each other, and she stood up, glancing at the darkening sky. "We'd better get back, or we'll be stumbling around in the dark."

"Fine. Rach? On our way back, could we just check the body?"

She looked quizzically at me and said, "Sure. We'd better take this path then." And she indicated a path striking off in a different direction.

We walked slowly. The wind and rain had probably obliterated the signs of my original entry into the woods, plus we were coming from the other direction, and that confused me. Finally I said, "Isn't this about it?" The woods were getting darker faster.

"I think so."

We found it almost at once; it was shadowy down in the ravine, and at first I thought we were in the wrong place because I couldn't see the body. But, as I ran my eyes up and down the ledge below us, I was pretty sure we were in the right place, and still— the body wasn't down there.

"Rachel?" I was whispering.

"What?" she whispered back.

"Is this the right place?"

"Yes. See? The rope I used to get down there this morning is still here." It didn't seem possible that it was just this morning that Aggie had found the body.

"But Rachel, do you see the body?" She shook her head, then went over and checked the rope where it was still tied around a tree. Apparently, she thought it was secure because she suddenly went over the side of the rift, startling me into voice, "Rachel!"

"I'll be right back." And she was. "I wanted to check further down. I thought maybe an animal had pushed him over the edge, and we just couldn't see it in the gloom."

"And?" Although I knew the answer already.

"There's no body down there."

We stared at each other for a minute, trying to take in the implications of the body disappearing. Then Rachel said, "Tyler, we've got to get going. It's getting dark."

She was right. We crashed through the woods to the path, not worrying about evidence anymore. We tried to hurry, but the deep black of a starless, moonless, forested night descended quickly. Rachel stopped abruptly, and I ran into her. The only thing I could see was her white face in the obsidian sea.

"Tyler. I'm going to take my shoes off because my bare feet will be able to recognize better if we leave the path. And I'm going to walk *very* slowly. If we step off this path . . . Well. You hold onto my sweater, so I don't have to worry about you, okay?"

I nodded, then realized she couldn't see it. "Yeah. Aggie?" I called softly, and Aggie pushed against my leg. "She's right here, Rach. I'm going to hold onto her collar to make sure she stays with us. I don't know if she can see any better than we can, but I don't want her wandering off, either."

"Okay, here we go."

I could tell she was putting one foot deliberately down in front of the other, every step being cautiously calculated. I was trying not to think of a murderer who'd moved the body and who might be near us. Who might even be creeping up behind me. Who might even have a gun in his hand. Or her hand.

Rachel stopped. "Did you see a light?" I was snuggling up against her, trying to move away from the "hacker" I knew was sneaking up behind me.

"No," but I was looking behind me, shivering a little.

We started moving again, very slowly, but she stopped again. "There is a light, Tyler. They must be out looking for us." Before I could say *wait! it might be the bogeyman* (or the real murderer), she called, "Hello! We're here! Hello! Are you out there?"

"Rachel? Tyler?" The voices floated back to us, and Rachel and I started yelling.

"Here we are! Here we are!" and to each other, "They're coming!" while Aggie barked at all the commotion.

In seconds, Mary Sharon was hugging us while Grace patted, first Rachel then me, on the back. "God we were terrified!" Mary Sharon's voice was wavering.

"We didn't know if you'd fallen over a cliff, gotten pushed, or just stayed out too long," Grace added.

"The others?" Rachel asked.

"We thought two of us should stay in the cabin and two should come out."

Mary Sharon finished, "Besides which, Julie made it clear she was not budging out of the cabin. Especially not with Grace."

"Jesus christ. We gotta get back. Rachel's barefoot."

"Barefoot?"

"It was the best way to ensure our staying on the path once it got so dark," Rachel explained.

With the flashlight, we made it back to the cabin in minutes. Teddie met us at the door. "Everybody okay?"

"We're fine," we assured her and got another round of hugs. Julie stood in the doorway to the living room but made no move to join us.

"We were scared!" Teddie said. "We didn't know what to think."

"I know. I'm sorry." I gave her another hug. "We just lingered too long . . ." Rachel and I exchanged glances.

Mary Sharon, of course, intercepted that look and demanded, "What?"

"A minute," I said, putting my hand up. "Rachel needs to get her feet warmed before she catches her death."

Teddie stirred the fire, and we wrapped Rachel in blankets. Grace sat on the coffee table in front of Rachel, took her feet in her hands, and rubbed them vigorously. I said, "Next time I'm going to be first and go barefoot."

"Aw, Sweetie," Mary Sharon moved behind my chair and rubbed my shoulders. "Are you feeling neglected?"

"Yeah. It was scary. I was bringing up the rear and the axe murderer was right behind me."

"Axe murderer!?" Julie's eyes were large and puzzled.

"You know," I brushed her drama away. "The 'bogeyman.' The one that you always knew, when you were a kid, was right behind you when you ran up the stairs in the dark?"

"Oh, him," she said, with obvious relief.

"Well, except . . ." Rachel looked at me. "There may actually be a bogeyman of some type out there."

"What?" Teddie asked.

"The body's gone."

"What?!" four voices exclaimed simultaneously.

"We went to check on it . . ."

"She was having a hunch, I think." Rachel indicated me.

I shrugged. "I don't know. I just thought we should, you know, check him out. He wasn't there."

"The rope was still there, so I went down to the ledge because I thought maybe an animal had rolled him off it, and he was just further down the ravine, but . . . nothing. The body's gone."

We stared at one another wordlessly. Then Julie got up and locked the front door and went into the kitchen, presumably to lock the back door. When she came back, she said, "Rachel? Do you have spotlights outside?"

Rachel shook her head. "Too much drain on the generator. We're on an island. The family never thought . . ." After a moment, she sat on the edge of her chair. "I need a drink. Anyone else? Or coffee? Hot chocolate? Something?"

Teddie pushed her back in her chair. "You stay. Get warm, Rachel. I'll get the drinks. What do you want? Some brandy?" Rachel nodded. Teddie looked around at the rest of us.

"Brandy sounds good," Julie said. "Is that okay, Tyler? I mean . . ."

"It's fine, Julie. Actually," I looked at Grace, "what do you say we get rip-roaring drunk, Grace?"

"A superb idea. You don't have any drugs with you, do you, Tyler? I really prefer drugs to liquor." I shook my head, and Grace went on, "No such luck, huh? Well, what about painkillers? Any of you have painkillers? They'll always do in a pinch."

"I might have some cough medicine in the bathroom," Rachel swung into the action.

Julie, her eyes large again, asked "You're really going to get drunk?"

I lowered my brows and stared at her.

"Jeez, Julie, they're kidding," Mary Sharon said. "You know, a little gallows humor?"

"Oh," Julie said.

"Actually, Teddie, hot chocolate sounds terrific."

"Yeah, I guess," Grace reluctantly agreed.

Mary Sharon said, "Come on, Teddie, I'll help."

In a few minutes, we were all settled in front of the fire again. I picked up the phone from the coffee table. Still nothing.

"Well," Teddie said, taking a sip of brandy, "what do you think is going on?" She looked around at us, apparently ready to entertain any theory.

"I don't know, Teddie. It does seem obvious that we have to assume there is someone else on this island with us."

"Why?"

"Well, this guy, this Jordan Blake, didn't just get up and walk away, Julie. So . . ."

"But it could've been you and Rachel tonight who moved him, for all we know."

I said evenly, carefully, "Yes. I guess it could've been."

"Jesus, Julie," Teddie said, "What is your problem?"

"Well, it *could've* happened that way, Teddie. You're all so intent on some outsider having done it, but what if Grace and Rachel did this together? Then they convinced Tyler—and this doesn't seem impossible to me at all—that it was justifiable homicide. Tonight they go out to get rid of the body, so there's really no evidence when we get the Coast Guard here tomorrow. I mean, it seems to me we could've flagged that ferry down tonight, but Rachel was set on waiting."

After a few minutes, Teddie said, "Or—I could've gotten rid of the body myself when I was out there alone earlier today."

"I went out once, too," Mary Sharon said, "so it might've been me."

Grace said, languidly, "Or me."

"You see?" Julie said.

"You just don't give up, do you?" Teddie said angrily. "Did you go out today?"

"No."

"But your gun's missing, and how do we know someone else wasn't doing *your* 'dirty work'?"

Julie snorted. "Like any of *you* would be helping *me.*"

"It wouldn't have to be one of us," Teddie pointed out.

"Can we stop this?" Rachel said, rubbing her fingertips into her eyeballs. "We have to assume that it is a possibility that one of us killed Jordan. It *is,*" she insisted when several of us shook our heads. "And we also have to assume that there *might* be someone else on this island with us. Someone who either came on with Jordan or after him. Who's also stranded since we haven't found a boat."

"Let's just review what we know," I said.

"Good," Mary Sharon agreed. "Let me write it down." She got up and found a notebook and pen.

"Ladies and ladies," I said with a flourish, "let me present Watson to my Sherlock."

"Sherlock Holmes was a cokehead," Grace said.

"Yep. That's true. First, we know that Grace had a less than agreeable run-in with Blake about a year ago. Right?" Grace nodded. "And that Rachel knew this guy from her youth, and he was trying to contact her before she came here. Yes?" Rachel nodded this time. "Okay. Rachel and Grace came to the island on Wednesday. What time did you arrive?"

"About noon," Rachel answered, looking at Grace, who nodded.

"And how did you get here?"

"Actually, we just hopped on a little seaplane on Lake Union in Seattle, which dropped us at Orcas. We keep the boat there. At the marina."

"Wait a minute," Mary Sharon insisted, as she wrote furiously.

"Mmm," I agreed. When she nodded, I continued. "So someone could actually have come here on a seaplane, too, right?" Rachel nodded. "Where would they land if they were going to do that?"

"In the bay, where the dock is. It's the only place where it's sheltered enough."

"Could someone do that without you hearing?"

Rachel thought for a minute. "Probably not. It's so close. Unless it was storming, in which case they wouldn't be out in a small plane nor able to land on a turbulent sea. But it makes me realize, there is another possibility, too."

"What?"

"On the northeast end of this island, there's a wide sand beach."

"Yeah, Mary Sharon and I saw it when we walked the perimeter today. There's no boat there though, if that's what you're thinking."

"No. What I was thinking is that a helicopter can land there. I did that once when the whole family was already here and I was late. The company has a helicopter, you see . . ."

"Mmmm," I said again. "More and more interesting. And presumably, Jordan Blake would have access to this helicopter?"

"Oh sure, it's his company now. And landing down on that beach? We'd never hear it from the house. Unless it flew right over the island. But if it came over sea and only approached the island as it was landing? No, we wouldn't hear it. Of course, it couldn't have been done during the storm . . ."

"Okay. So Jordan—and another interloper—must have come before the storm, either by boat, which left after dropping them off or was torn away during the storm. Or by plane (not likely because it would've been heard) or by helicopter. Of course, they might have come before you two even arrived. Did you do any wandering around on the island the couple of days you were here before us?" Both Rachel and Grace shook their heads. "Oh yeah, you already told us that, didn't you? If we assume someone else, not one of us, murdered Jordan, they might have come together, had a disagreement . . ."

"The classic 'falling out of thieves'?"

"Something like that," I shrugged. "And the murderer or survivor of the fight, whatever, got away on the boat or helicopter they'd come on. Except. Now that the body's been moved, we have to assume this other person or persons is still on the island, without means of getting off."

"But they might get off tonight, now that the storm has subsided, if they have a way to signal someone?"

"Maybe. But all this is speculation, and I really want to try and stick with what we *know*. So. The rest of us arrive together on Friday about three o'clock. The storm is breaking as we arrive. For hours, we are stranded by this squall and otherwise engaged, anyway. We are not out of one another's eyes."

"Except for the occasional trip to the bathroom."

"Right," I agreed. "And during those hours—does anyone have any idea what time it was when Teddie saw the figure outside?"

"We were eating," Grace said. "About seven-thirty or eight?"

Others nodded. "So about seven-thirty, Teddie saw someone outside the cabin. We don't know who that person was, but it was probably a man. Is that right, Teddie?" She nodded. "It could've been Jordan Blake, or it could've been his accomplice or murderer. All we know for sure was there was something suspicious about this person because it was a horrible tempest, and he didn't ask for shelter.

"Then we went to bed. At this point, we can't much guarantee what anyone's activity was. I slept in the same bed with Mary Sharon, and I'm certain that I would've noticed if she'd gotten up in the night. She did not."

I looked at Mary Sharon, and she smiled weakly. "Well, I'm afraid I can't provide an alibi for you, Tyler. I sleep like the dead—eeuuuw, bad choice of words—and I probably wouldn't have noticed if you'd brought someone to bed with you."

"Someone did get up and go downstairs from the other room sometime during the night," I said, pausing a minute to think. "Or it could be that I heard them coming back to the bedroom, I guess. I only heard one trip; presumably either I was asleep when they went down the stairs and heard them coming back, or I fell asleep after they went downstairs and didn't hear them return. No, wait. I heard a door open before I heard someone on the steps, so I heard them go down but not back up."

"That was me," Julie said. "I went down to the bathroom. And I'm a very light sleeper, so I think I would have heard anyone getting up from either bedroom upstairs. No one did."

Teddie shrugged. "I sleep pretty soundly. And Friday? I flew in from D.C., so I was tired, besides which—what time did we go to bed? About eleven?" Nods. "That makes it about 2 a.m. my time. I just dropped off and remember nothing until Mary Sharon was waking me in the morning."

I looked at Rachel and Grace. "We slept in the same bed, too," Grace responded. "I don't sleep well. I got up at least twice, maybe three times."

"To do what?"

"I peed once. The other time," she shrugged, "I didn't do anything. I was just restless, prowled around for a little bit. Raided the refrigerator. Rachel didn't get up all night. I heard one person come down the stairs, and they went back up, almost at once. I heard the toilet flush." She spread her hands. "That's it."

Rachel said, "And I just slept. I'm sorry, but I don't remember a thing after my head hit the pillow."

"So," I resumed my summation. "When I came down in the morning, about 6 a.m., Rachel was in the kitchen. I took Aggie for her walk and discovered the body. I came back, and Mary Sharon and Grace were up. After I told them about my discovery, Mary Sharon woke Julie and Teddie, and we all went to look at the body. There was a bullet hole in Blake's back, and when Rachel turned him over, it was clear that Grace knew him." I paused and thought for a minute. "When we left the murder site, presuming it happened there, Julie was missing."

We all looked at her, and she said defensively, "I already told you! I was anxious to see if the boat was intact, so we could get off the island in a hurry. I just went to check on the boat, that's all."

"Which it wasn't," I continued. "Intact, I mean. It was gone. Later, Mary Sharon and I discovered the boat with two or three holes in it, which could have been done deliberately but could just as easily have happened because of the sea smashing the boat against the rocks."

"Give me a minute," Mary Sharon requested again, and I waited while she scribbled quickly. Finally, she said, "Okay. Go ahead."

"So then we discover that Julie has a gun with her, but it's missing. And Grace and Rachel both know this Jordan Blake. But no one else seems to know him. At first." I looked around at the circle of faces, giving them an opportunity to contradict me. "Blake could be angry at either Rachel or Grace, for past slights. But also, he might have been trying to see Rachel—some business idea he had.

"Of course, later we find out that Julie and Teddie have some knowledge of this man, too. In fact, Teddie's told him she's coming out to this island, that the island is owned by the Finebergs, that she and Rachel are old friends, maybe she even told him our names, and she's meeting with him after our get-together. During the day, some time or other, everyone but Julie leaves the cabin. And finally, at about nine o'clock this evening—" I glance at Rachel.

"Probably a little later. Judging by how soon it got dark."

"So maybe closer to nine-thirty, Rachel and I discover the body is missing." I look at everyone again. "That about sums it up. Did I leave anything out? Anyone want to add anything?"

"Yeah," Julie said. "If it's not an outsider and if we assume it happened sometime Friday night—let me look at that a minute, Mary Sharon," she held her hand out for the notebook, which Mary Sharon relinquished to her.

"It's messy," Mary Sharon explained. "I have to make it more readable."

Julie nodded, her eyes running down the list, then looked up at us and said, reluctantly, "Then we have to assume it's Grace who did it."

"What?" Teddie exclaimed. "This isn't Clue, Julie. Professor Plum did it with a knife in the library."

"For christ's sake!" Rachel exploded.

"Julie . . ." I protested.

She put a hand up. "Just listen, will you? After we all went to bed, Grace clearly describes her night as being restless and characterizes herself as not being a good sleeper. She heard one person come down the stairs, pee, and go back up the stairs. That's all. All night. She's made it clear: the only person who could've gotten out to kill Blake would have been her."

No one said anything for a minute. Then Grace said succinctly, "She's right. Even though I *didn't* do it, I am the only one who *could've*—assuming it was done that night."

"Except you could be lying to protect someone else," I suggested. "You see? There's just no way to know."

"**O**h, I give up," Teddie stood up and threw her hands in the air. "No matter how logical we are, how thorough, we can't figure this out! We're obviously missing some puzzle pieces!"

"I agree," Rachel said, also standing. "I'm going to bed."

"Wait!" Julie insisted. "Don't you think we should take turns staying awake, standing watch?"

"All night?"

"There's six of us. We can each take an hour and a half. That way, if someone tries to do something or get off the island, we'll know."

"But would you feel safe with me taking a turn?" Grace asked slyly.

"Or me?" Rachel added.

Julie looked doubtful, and I said, "Forget it, Julie. It's just not going to work."

"Well, I guess not. But . . ." she hesitated a minute, looking at the couch, then turning to look at the curtainless windows. "I think I'll sleep on the couch tonight."

None of us said anything for a minute, then Rachel shrugged. "Suit yourself, Julie. You'll have to strip the sheets and pillow and quilt from your bed upstairs because there's no extra bedding."

We all started our nighttime ablutions. "Come on, Aggie," I said, taking her out the back door. I hugged the house while she ventured a little ways to the edge of the clearing; I could barely see her in the light from the kitchen and was somewhat comforted by the muffled noises from the interior of the cabin. "Do your stuff, Aggie. Hurry up." My eyes were scanning the dark woods.

After Aggie squatted, she turned toward the trees and stared intently, lifting her ears. "Don't do that!" I protested. "You're just freaking me out." She started to growl. "Aggie!" I said sharply, opening the door. She followed me in.

Mary Sharon was in the kitchen, waiting her turn for the bathroom. "What's the matter?" she asked.

"Why?"

"I heard you snap at Aggie, and you look jumpy."

"Aggie was just doing that *thing* she does—you know, she stares at something and growls. It might be a spider, for christ's sake, but it always makes me feel there's a rapist or something out there. And now . . ."

Mary Sharon bent over and scratched the obliging Aggie's ears. "Are you going to be our protector, Agatha?"

Often, as I float in that idyllic place halfway between sleep and wakefulness, I hear someone call my name. A therapist once told me that it was probably just me, reaching out to myself, giving myself a wake-up call, so to speak. *Whatever that means,* I'd said crabbily to Mary Sharon.

So, at first, when someone was whispering "Tyler?" I paid no attention, thinking it was just me, as usual. However, when it continued, like an annoying mosquito, I finally reacted.

"What?" I said, feeling stupid because I thought I was answering myself.

"Someone's out there, Tyler."

It was Julie, not me. I came fully awake. "What?" I repeated.

"Someone's out there."

"What time is it?"

"Just after four."

I sat up. "Mary Sharon?" I prodded her with my foot. "What do you mean, Julie? Did you see someone?" I could make out her dark figure, crouching by the side of my bed. Aggie's tail was swishing back and forth on the wood floor. I jabbed Mary Sharon again and said, a little louder, "Mary Sharon."

"Yes," Julie continued to whisper. "I was dozing on and off when I had this sensation that someone was looking at me." I felt a shiver slither down my spine and glanced at our window, knowing full well that no one could be looking in these second-story windows. "My eyes were closed, so I opened them just a slit, so it would look like they were still closed. That was how certain I was that someone was looking at me. At the window, I could see a face peering in, a pale blur for just a minute. I didn't move."

"Mary Sharon," I said out loud. Then I leaned over and spoke directly in her ear. "Flood!" It was a dirty trick, but I knew it would work. When she was a little girl, the river in her hometown had flooded, and she'd seen a cousin swept away in the maelstrom. She'd had a morbid fear of floods ever since.

"What?" she jumped to a sitting position immediately.

"There's someone outside. Come on, we have to investigate."
She stared at me as if she didn't comprehend, and I began again,
"Mary Sharon . . ."

"You do it," she interrupted me and snuggled back under her
covers.

I capitulated. Julie went back downstairs as I pulled clothes on
hastily. When I crept out of the bedroom, turning no lights on, I
bumped into another human. I screamed. So did Teddie, and we
clung to one another, giggling.

Mary Sharon mumbled but didn't get up. "I guess we woke
you, huh?"

"Yeah. 'Flood'?"

"It always wakes Mary Sharon."

"Not this time, apparently." We were padding down the
staircase.

"No, it did wake her. She just refused to stay awake."

Grace came out of her bedroom, fully dressed, as we reached
the bottom of the stairs. Julie jumped when she saw her.

"You heard it?" Grace asked. "Someone outside?"

Julie, recovering her equilibrium, nodded. "I saw someone, a
face peeking in the living room window."

"What are we going to do?"

"I don't know," I admitted. "I don't think we can go outside. If
it's the murderer, he has a gun." We hadn't turned lights on, our
eyes getting used to the dark. We were huddled in the kitchen
where there was only one high window. None of us wanted to go
into the living room, with its immense walls of uncurtained glass. I
peeked in there, though, looking outside. The sky was just
beginning to move toward a chalky grey.

"So we're just going to do nothing?" Grace asked, fidgeting.

"Grace, we have no weapons."

"Not entirely true. *I* have my gun." Julie pulled a small
handgun out of her jeans pocket. We stared, speechless, at her. "I'm

sorry, but I didn't know who to trust and who not to trust. I wasn't turning my gun over to anyone. Not knowing what they might want it for or how they might use it." We were still speechless, and she continued, "Don't you see? I know, now, that someone else is out there, but—until I saw that face at the window—I wasn't convinced. For all I knew, if I gave my gun to Rachel, I might be giving it to a killer. Not that I *really* thought she was a killer, but I had no way of knowing for sure."

It made a kind of sense, I guess, but I was still horrified that Julie could be this mistrusting of us. I could almost feel the heat of Teddie's anger next to me. At that moment, Rachel entered the room and stopped, sucking in her breath, at the sight of Julie with a gun in her hand, looking as if she were pointing it toward the three of us. Julie immediately grasped the picture through Rachel's eyes and switched the gun to her left hand, holding it by its barrel. "It's okay, Rachel. I'm just holding this gun."

Rachel looked at us, and we nodded. "What's going on?" We brought her up to date. "I don't think we should go out," she said firmly. "It's too risky, and too little is likely to be accomplished."

The room was getting lighter, and I caught a look of doubt crossing Julie's face. I wondered if she was thinking that Rachel might be aiding an accomplice to escape. *Wait a minute. Was I wondering that myself?*

Just as Rachel started to make coffee, the other four of us still huddled in the kitchen with her, we heard a racket overhead. We looked at one another, knowing the sound. We rushed outside and saw a helicopter thundering overhead. Aggie barked ferociously while Mary Sharon slept through it all.

In a way, that's the end of the story. There's lots more *details,* of course, but few more facts. Rachel's cellular phone never did work. The Coast Guard showed up after we signalled the ferry with flares on Sunday morning. After we told our story, they called in the San Juan County sheriff, who in turn eventually called in the Washington State Patrol.

A "camp" was found, deep in the woods between paths, where it appeared that at least two people had been staying. There was evidence of a good-sized tent and cooking equipment, all gone now. The latrine pit indicated that there'd been someone at this camp for some time, not just over the weekend. It was hard for the six of us to imagine anyone staying in a tent through that downpour on Friday night and part of Saturday. As far as I know (the police, after all, don't tell us potential suspects everything), there was never any discovery of who'd been using this camp and why. There were some theories, of course. And we did get *some* information from a friend of a friend of Grace's, in the police department.

Blood was found embedded in the soil on the ledge where Aggie'd discovered Blake's body. It must've seeped into the ground, protected from the storm by his own body. It matched Blake's blood type all right, but without a body, a more conclusive ID was never made. Blake was, of course, missing. He'd left his office on Thursday afternoon, after jocularly telling his v.p./assistant that he was going to "settle an old score." He's never been seen since. And no body has ever been recovered.

We all wondered, among ourselves, if his body had been taken up in the helicopter and then just dumped into the sea somewhere. Rachel, especially, thought that was most likely because if someone just threw it off one of the island's cliffs, it almost for sure would've washed back up on the island itself. Or a nearby island. Unless, of course, he'd been weighted down, Teddie had pointed out.

Northland Lumber had records indicating that its helicopter had been signed out by Blake on Thursday evening and Saturday evening. Quite impossible, of course, at least the second time. No one at the airport, conveniently or not, had any memory of what the person looked like who'd actually signed the helicopter out or if there'd been more than one person, either time.

Most other evidence had been thoroughly obliterated by the storm that had lasted the better part of twenty-four hours.

We were all questioned exhaustively, collectively and separately, at the island and for two days following, on the mainland. That morning, before we sent up our flares, we talked about what we'd tell the cops. Teddie and I thought we should leave Grace's part out, that it would probably never surface anyway, although Rachel's connection was sure to be found out, so we'd have to admit to knowing that.

Julie, of course, was indignant. "I can't do that! Lie to the police? You're crazy to even ask me to do that!"

Mary Sharon shook her head. "I'm sorry, but I've got to side with Julie on this one. I think we have to tell the whole truth. The chances of them finding out are always there, and then it would look even worse. Besides, as an officer of the court, I'm obligated to tell everything I know."

"Oh, for heaven's sakes, Mary Sharon," I said disgustedly, "you're not 'an officer of the court' in the state of Washington."

"No, Tyler, but I do have to uphold the law everywhere."

I rolled my eyes. It was a long-standing argument between us: this issue of the law versus extenuating circumstances plus the real meaning of the word "justice." But Grace herself eliminated the disagreement. "Mary Sharon is absolutely right. If we don't tell the whole truth and any of it ever comes out, the suspicion will land on me heavier than ever. Best to be honest."

So Grace and Rachel both told the truth of their connection with Jordan Blake, and the rest of us told what little we knew and answered questions about what we'd been told, when asked.

After all our agonizing, the police were never very interested in Grace's and Rachel's connections with Jordan Blake. And dismissed Julie and Teddie as unimportant. They were obviously convinced that the big business/big media aspects of Blake's life were more likely suspect than a couple of negligible moments spent with a couple of neligible women or any other tenuous ties.

"In other words," Rachel said, "any six women like ourselves could kill a well-placed man and get away with it because no self-respecting police officer would believe that we could be taken seriously as suspects."

"Yup," Mary Sharon quipped. "We're clearly not 'the usual suspects'!"

Julie's husband, Tony, flew out to be with her. He seemed okay. He was a little wary of the five of us but appeared to be genuinely devoted to Julie. It was hard for me, after all we'd been through together that weekend and then seeing Julie and Tony together, to even imagine Julie and *me* together, to even have the slightest comprehension of why I'd been carrying a torch for this woman for seventeen years. Of course, I know it was the fantasy of Julie-as-her-college-self that I was carrying the torch for. And maybe, I suddenly realized, the torch was for me—for my youthful self, so full of optimism and faith. And booze. I felt sad that Julie had changed so much and oddly relieved, too. But I also understood something completely different: I realized I felt sad, at least partly, because I no longer had this stupidly comfortable but warmly familiar grudge to nurse. It made me feel disoriented, but also a little freer.

After a couple of days, the police told us that we could leave, all but Rachel and Grace, demanding we make ourselves available, if necessary. Because Mary Sharon and I had planned to drive back to Minnesota and were not on a tight deadline of any sort, we decided to stay for a few days.

The farewell at the airport was a little uncomfortable. Julie's plane left first. Tony was smart enough to go ahead and get on without her, giving us a moment alone. We stood around awkwardly, not knowing what to say or do. Julie looked dejected, and I felt sorry for her.

"Well," she said with a cheerfully brittle voice, "I can't say it's been a swell time." We all laughed, hollowly. "But Rachel, thank you for doing this for us. I think it's . . . well, for me at least, it's laid a ghost or two to rest." She smiled tentatively in my direction, and I responded in kind. *I'll say,* I echoed silently in my mind. "And really, it was great seeing you guys again." After a little pause, she added, "Mostly."

Teddie, who had seemed to be the angriest at Julie all weekend, surprised me by going to Julie first and enveloping her in a big hug. We all followed her lead, not saying much. When Julie left to get on the plane, she didn't look back, although it was clear she was wiping her eyes.

"Whew!" Teddie said, when she was out of sight. "I suspect we'll never see her again."

"It's sad," Grace said. "It's not like we've lost her or she's lost us. It's like she's lost herself." We walked, thoughtfully, to Teddie's gate.

"And all that history we shared," I sighed wistfully.

"And laughs! Remember the time she mooned those CIA guys who were on campus recruiting?" Rachel said.

"Oh yeah. And it was her idea that we have those bumper stickers made up—*This Man Frequents Porn Shops*—that we then stuck on the cars of men who were going into the porn places on Lake Street. Remember?" Teddie added.

"And don't forget my senior project!" Mary Sharon reminded us. "Julie's the one who thought up the idea of making breast-prints and butt-prints to symbolize the transformation of women's bodies from passive objects in art to active agents in art."

"And I loved her," I reminded them. They all patted me on the arms or back.

"Yup," Teddie said. "Those were the days. You know, it pisses me off. We should have been doing this all weekend instead of . . ."

"Suspecting one another?" Grace supplied.

"Yeah. Now we have to have another reunion."

"But Julie?" Mary Sharon looked at each of us, and we—in turn—looked at one another, shrugging or shaking our heads.

Rachel said, "You know, she probably wouldn't come anyway, but . . ."

"I agree," I jumped in. "I think we should invite her."

There was a silence, then Teddie said, "Actually, I know people much worse than Julie. We probably just had high expectations of her, because of our past."

"As far as that goes," Grace said, "how about no Tyler? I mean, isn't she the one who keeps finding dead bodies?"

"Good point," Rachel agreed.

"So Mary Sharon, can you have us all at your B & B without inviting Tyler?"

"I think so," she agreed.

"Hey! I object! You can't do this without me!"

"Why not?" Grace asked.

"Because . . . because you might need someone to get stuff down from the high shelves." They always told me that was the only reason they let me live with them.

"Well," Teddie agreed, "it's true, we *might* need her."

"And you know," Mary Sharon added, "you haven't heard her Stony River stories. You think *I* got stories!"

"Oh, no!" Grace groaned. "More hometown stories?"

We slipped our arms around one another, subsiding into giddy silliness. Our affection had been put on hold all weekend. By the time Teddie left, we'd exchanged e-mail addresses and faxes (all except Grace, who said she was still resisting the age of technology) and real-mail addresses and phone numbers and had set a tentative date for getting together the next summer at Mary Sharon's.

The newspapers in the Seattle area were having a field day.

NORTHLAND LUMBER EXEC MISSING
WOMEN SAY HE WAS MURDERED

The headlines were all variations of this. Several theories emerged about what had happened to him. Almost none of them involved us. It turned out that he was, indeed, in a deadly fight with a hostile takeover action. Most of the company, even the other execs, thought it was a good idea, but Blake was fighting it savagely because, according to the general consensus, he would be sacked if it were successful. And the major instigator of the takeover was an old prep school classmate and rival of Blake's, so the cryptic remark about "settling an old score" could have been in reference to this person.

But the camp in the woods, mostly, remained a mystery. The major theory about it was that it was used by an environmental group. Northland had recently landed a contract that would actually allow it to do some select clear-cutting on some of the untenanted islands in the San Juans, the first major lumbering on the islands since the 1800s. So, the thinking went, an environmental group had been using this camp as a takeoff place for some of their protests, plenty of which had been occurring on other islands during the months preceding our reunion. But nothing was ever proven. And the "settling an old score" could just as easily pertain to these groups since Blake had been battling with some of these individuals for twenty or more years. Of course, for that matter, it could have been a reference to either Rachel or Grace, too.

Jordan Blake's disappearance and "alleged murder"—as the papers always put it—was never solved, just went down in that long list of unsolved murders.

As Mary Sharon, "the officer of the court," pointed out, "It's only on TV and in mystery books that the murderer is always caught. The vast majority of real murders remain unsolved and, in fact, in many cases, go entirely undetected."

I sometimes wonder if this murder might have gone undetected if it weren't for all of us, but especially Aggie, being on the island that weekend. If Aggie hadn't found the body, if we all hadn't seen it, wouldn't Blake have just disappeared?

The consequence of the police's indifference about Grace's connection to Jordan Blake was that her business went on, unperturbed. The consequences for Rachel were a little different. Although no cloud of suspicion hung over her head, the island was never quite paradise again, never the haven of safety and serenity it had always been to her. The spectre of violence taints places as well as people.

The rest of us, I guess, went on with our lives. We have invited Julie to the next reunion, although she hasn't responded yet. The rest of us all intend to be there "with bells on," as Grace says. It will be her first trip back to Minnesota in years.

It's easy for me to picture Julie's life as truncated, head-in-the-sand oblivion, but that's probably not fair. The truth is, she is active in AIDS and sexual harassment, neither inconsequential issues. Each of us has to choose our own way, find our own method of survival and activism. I could not feel safe or content unless I was "storming the barricades"—making a concerted effort to change the deep disease of oppression endemic in this society. Others do it other ways.

Certainly Teddie continues to do it through her brilliant guiding of the foundation she runs, which continues to find dazzling ways to improve the world. And also through her efforts to raise daughters who will take their place in the world of activism. We keep in closer touch now, have even visited each other and initiated careful conversations about the possibility of successful long-distance relationships. I admit I feel increasingly dizzy in Teddie's presence, but I am moving with great caution, not being able to imagine how to work out the logistics of such an alliance. And not being sure I want to risk such a commitment, anyway. To anyone. The woman I'd been dating when I left for the reunion, Jill, did use my absence to fade out of my life, as I had predicted.

Rachel, too, with her clinic and strong commitment to women's and children's issues, lives her feminism. And, in her own unique way, so does Grace.

Mary Sharon continues with her deep love of Minnesota, justice, and Celia—not necessarily in that order. She changes lives by merely being herself: a slightly subdued, slightly aging radical-feminist-lesbian attorney, activist, neighbor in a small town/rural county.

And I continue doing it my way, too. By writing, by being politically active, by serving in organizations committed to feminist social change, by loving women in a variety of ways. My second novel will soon be out. I still straddle the passion and roots

I have in urban California and the home of my family in rural northern Minnesota, not wanting yet to give anything up.

Mary Sharon, Teddie, and I have talked endlessly about that weekend on the island—examined it, changed our minds about it, tried to make sense of it. None of us have talked to Grace and Rachel directly. I'm not sure we want to. I guess, in some remote corner of my mind, I will always wonder if Grace—and maybe Grace and Rachel together—got away with murder. And I wonder, if they did, if I mind. And I wonder, honestly, what that means about who I am.

More Spinsters Ink Titles
from the
Feminist Mystery Series

Spinsters titles are available at your local booksellers or by mail order through Spinsters Ink. A free catalog is available upon request. Please include $2.00 for the first title ordered and 50¢ for every title thereafter. Visa and Mastercard accepted.

Spinsters Ink
32 E. First St., #330
Duluth, MN 55802-2002
USA

218-727-3222 (phone)   (fax) 218-727-3119
(e-mail) spinster@spinsters-ink.com
(website) http://www.spinsters-ink.com

Spinsters Ink was founded in 1978 to produce vital books for diverse women's communities. In 1986 we merged with Aunt Lute Books to become Spinsters/Aunt Lute. In 1990, the Aunt Lute Foundation became an independent nonprofit publishing program. In 1992, Spinsters moved to Minnesota.

Spinsters Ink publishes novels and nonfiction works that deal with significant issues in women's lives from a feminist perspective: books that not only name these crucial issues, but—more important—encourage change and growth. We are committed to publishing works by women writing from the periphery: fat women, Jewish women, lesbians, old women, poor women, rural women, women examining classism, women of color, women with disabilities, women who are writing books that help make the best in our lives more possible.

JOAN M. DRURY

For part of the year, I live in a house on a sand spit that protrudes some six miles into Lake Superior—creating the harbor in Duluth, Minnesota that is the fourth largest international port in the United States. My house is nestled in a grove of mature red and jack pines, maples, fruit trees, and mountain ash on the edge of undulating sand dunes that stretch the entire length of this island. Although right in the city, it feels like it is in the north woods on the edge of an ocean.

I cross the aerial lift bridge connecting this plot of land to the mainland of Duluth and go to work every day at the Building for Women—a building owned by and populated by women's organizations. My offices, also, overlook this most astonishing of lakes and the shipping traffic—an incredible view of which I never tire. These enormous ships, some of them bound to the Great Lakes (lakers) while some are oceangoing (salties), are sometimes a city block or two long and never fail to delight me.

I oversee the operations of Spinsters Ink, a feminist publishing company, and Harmony Women's Fund, a private foundation that funds women's activities resulting in feminist social change in the state of Minnesota. I'm also involved in many other feminist endeavors. I can only do what I do and as much as I do because I work with a group of women who are exceptionally talented and capable, dedicated and supportive.

The rest of the year I live on seven quiet acres in Lutsen, Minnesota, some ninety miles northeast of Duluth. This is a small town, mostly rural, on the edge of a million acres of wilderness on one side and the largest fresh-water sea in the world, Lake Superior, on the other. The sand dunes of my city home are replaced by wild, rugged, rocky shores. I share this location with gulls, eagles, bears, wolves, deer, chipmunks, and many other wildlife creatures. The almost-claustrophobic closeness of the tight forest gives way abruptly to the limitless horizon of endless and ever-changing water—creating, for me, a metaphoric and exhilarating clash of cultures.

Next door to me is Norcroft: A Writing Retreat for Women—a special project of Harmony Women's Fund—where four women, at a time, come to its ten acres to write. This gives me a kind of built-in community along with the good-hearted people who live in this area and who have been welcoming me back all my life. My dear and beloved friends, my daughter and two sons, my daughter-by-marriage, and my granddaughters all come to visit me and share my glorious existence.

Here, in the serenity of semi-isolation and unutterable beauty, I write—and read, talk, think, solve problems, dream, breathe.